CAST A DEADLY SHADOW

Four men went up into the mountains in search of a lost mine. Only one came back — insane with fear. Old Colonel Fogarty wanted to know what happened. No one seemed willing to find out, except his daughter, Rachel. She was joined by the colonel's mean-tempered surveyor, Harvey Wheeler, two locals with their own larcenous plans . . . and Jason Hart, a stranger whose job was 'chasing shadows'. But what were his intentions when the mountain's dark secrets were finally unlocked?

STEVE HAYES AND
DAVID WHITEHEAD

CAST A DEADLY SHADOW

Complete and Unabridged

LINFORD
Leicester

First published in Great Britain in 2011

First Linford Edition
published 2012

Copyright © 2011 by Steve Hayes and
David Whitehead

British Library CIP Data

Hayes, Steve.
    Cast a deadly shadow. - -
    (Linford mystery library)
    1. Suspense fiction.
    2. Large type books.
    I. Title II. Series III. Whitehead, David,
    1958–
    823.9′2–dc23

    ISBN 978–1–4448–1041–7

Published by
F. A. Thorpe (Publishing)
Anstey, Leicestershire

Set by Words & Graphics Ltd.
Anstey, Leicestershire
Printed and bound in Great Britain by
T. J. International Ltd., Padstow, Cornwall

This book is printed on acid-free paper

'An open mind is the cornerstone of life'

— *Anonymous*

1

In the old days they would have packed all their supplies and equipment aboard a string of mules, and the men themselves would have taken to the saddle. Even then it would have been a difficult climb. But this was 1929, so they did things the modern way instead — which meant piling everyone and everything into Colonel Fogarty's bright blue Studebaker touring car and using horsepower of a different kind.

Ahead of them the Jemez Mountains — the great, roughly-circular sprawl of canyons and mesas that dominated Sandoval County, New Mexico — lifted toward the sky in a series of green and ochre-colored crags. Beyond those peaks lay a patchwork of rock and stream, meadow and forest — and quite possibly a king's ransom in gold, silver, copper and pumice.

Behind the steering wheel, Perry

Tucker stared off into the distance and pondered the long trek before them. As Colonel Fogarty's chief surveyor, it was his job to find the mother lode — if it existed at all. His assistant, Lester Moore, sat beside him, fanning himself with a photostatic copy of the map the colonel had acquired in somewhat less than clear circumstances. In back, wedged up against all the gear they couldn't fit into the trunk, sat two tougher-looking men who had been hired as combination guides and bodyguards, for the colonel had been reluctant to send his two best surveyors up into the wilderness without protection. These were Tom Ross and Battista Bianchi.

The car's white-walled tires continued to bounce over the uneven, brush-choked plain, the growl and occasional pop of its six-cylinder engine forging out ahead of it, as did Bianchi's deep, operatic voice as he sang *Prisoner of Love.*

'*Someone that I belong to . . . Doesn't belong to me . . . Someone who can't be faithful . . . Knows that I have to be . . .* '

Tucker glanced at Moore and allowed

himself a fleeting smile. Thin and feminine beneath his Panama hat and open-necked white shirt, Moore was twisted around in his seat, watching Bianchi with open admiration. The slim Italian, with his dark, curly hair and battered but likeable face, had enchanted him from the first, and it seemed to Tucker that Moore had already fallen hopelessly in love with him.

Sure enough, when Bianchi finished the song Moore burst into spontaneous applause. A man's man all the way through, Tom Ross eyed the effeminate surveyor's assistant with open distaste. But Bianchi, who always enjoyed being the center of attention, tipped his head graciously, acknowledging Moore's appreciation.

None of them had any idea they were being watched from the far-off mountains, nor that the watcher had seen enough of them and their equipment to form a clear conclusion as to their purpose here.

The watcher — stocky and brown-skinned, his shoulder-length black hair tied down beneath a greasy headband — uncoiled slowly from the rocks in which he had taken cover, collapsed his ancient telescope, then turned and set off back into the hills at a lope. Bidziil had to know about this. Or, more accurately, since Bidziil already knew everything anyway, he had to have his suspicions confirmed.

Then he could act accordingly.

★   ★   ★

As dusk fell, the old Navajo Indian sat cross-legged and for long, silent moments stared hard at the ground before him. Bidziil was old now, and had been old for as long as even the oldest of his people could remember. Short and thickset, with long, center-parted hair as gray as smoke, his wrinkled prune of a face was home to black, deep-sunk eyes, a long, hooked nose and fleshy lips pinched down at the corners.

After a moment the shaman's wrinkled hands set to work, for that's what Bidziil was — a *Hatalii,* in his own language; one who could bridge the gap between this world and the next, and practice sorcery, healing and divination with equal skill.

By the uncertain light of the torches held high by his *diné* — his people — he took up handfuls of sand and let them trickle through his fists like the grains in an hourglass. With crushed gypsum and yellow ochre he worked; with red sandstone, charcoal and brightly-colored flower pollen. He labored slowly and silently, showing meticulous attention to detail, and over time the lines began to join up and fill in and hint at a specific shape — that of the great trickster himself; the dark magician, the thief, the First Scolder . . . Maii', the shape-shifter, the skin-walker.

Around him his people began to chant softly in prayer, and as the wind picked up it tore at the torch-flames but, curiously, left the sand painting completely undisturbed. Shadows capered around Bidziil's audience, and they themselves took on an unreal aspect beneath the restless amber light.

Then, all at once, the image in the sand became so clear that there could be no mistaking it for anything other than what it was; a hulking figure that was part-man, part-wolf, a beast in skins who came from the darkness to hunt and kill in order to serve and protect.

Maii'.

Coyote.

His work finished, Bidziil finally closed his eyes and his lips started working in murmured prayer. His old, bent-backed body rocked in time to the slow, potent metronome of his words. His head craned back, his eyelids flickered open again and he stared up at the clear night sky.

Silence fell, abrupt and complete. There was no longer any moan of wind or snap of fire, *nothing*. Bidziil and his people waited expectantly, and after a while the wind picked up again, carrying to them a strange sound, something like a gust of air passing through a wooden instrument, perhaps a flute . . . and yet not like that at all.

A new shadow joined those already there — the merest shimmer of fluid, gray-black movement half-seen from the corner of an eye, gone almost before it could register.

Bidziil smiled.
It was done.
Maii' had been summoned.
And once summoned, he would kill.

2

Bianchi's voice echoed through the high country.

'*Your eyes so blue . . . Your kisses, too . . . I never knew what they could do . . . I can't believe you're in love with —* '

'Say, what's that?'

It was mid-morning of the following day, and Perry Tucker's party was well into the mountains now, though it had been a struggle to get even this far in the Studebaker. Ross had been right, back in Jemez Springs. He'd said the hills weren't built for cars. Horses and mules were the way to go. But Tucker had worked for Colonel Fogarty so long now that he guessed some of the colonel's stubbornness had rubbed off on him. Besides, the colonel had insisted they take the car, and he was used to having his own way.

Still, the hills had rapidly become a source of wonder to Tucker. He'd expected to find a wilderness of rock and not much else. Instead he'd discovered a wonderland of lakes and waterfalls, winding streams and lush meadows, and great belts of ponderosa pine and Douglas fir.

Of course, between all that there had been rock a-plenty; twisting canyons and switchbacks, slopes too rough or too steep to negotiate, and vast walls of varicolored sandstone, their tops black with ancient accumulations of volcanic ash known as *tuff*. But overall, the mountains had been a revelation to him, a place of beauty and tranquility.

Only after dark did the true isolation of the high country make itself known. They'd all felt it last night, even Ross and Bianchi, and by mutual if unspoken agreement had bedded down early in an effort to sleep it away.

When Tucker finally crawled out of his small tent at sunrise he'd found Moore crouching beside the fire, ostensibly fixing coffee but actually staring open-mouthed at Bianchi, who had stripped off and was scrubbing himself down in one of the hot pools that littered the region. Moore had hardly been able to take his eyes off the naked Italian, and watching him struggling to appear so casual and disinterested amused Tucker no end.

Bianchi kept them entertained throughout the morning. He never tired of singing, and Moore never tired of listening to him. But finally something off to one side of the rocky trail caught Moore's eye, he called, 'Say, what's that?' and Tucker quickly brought the Studebaker to a jolting stop.

'What's *what?*' he asked.

Without bothering to answer, Moore climbed out and hustled back along the trail. Tucker and the others, curious to know what he'd seen, immediately got out and followed him.

When they caught up, Moore was standing over a sand painting. They gathered around and stared down at it. It was about two feet square, and seemed to show some kind of strange-looking creature that looked similar to a dog, but which was standing on its hind legs.

'What is it?' asked Moore.

'A warning,' growled Ross.

Moore smiled, thinking he was joking.

'No. What is it *really?*'

'I just told you,' said Ross.

Moore's smile faded. 'Well, who put it there? Who's it meant to warn . . . and why?'

'How should I know?'

'Well . . . is it meant for *us*, do you suppose?'

'I doubt it,' Ross replied without much conviction. 'Nobody knew we were coming, right?'

'But if there's someone else up here and they — '

'I said don't worry about it,' said Ross, his tone sharper now.

They all looked at the warning for a while longer. The near-constant wind dropped suddenly and the high country fell quiet. There was no drop in temperature. If anything, it grew a little warmer. And yet Perry Tucker had to suppress a shiver.

'All right,' he said, finally breaking the moment. 'Let's move on.'

They headed back to the car, but Tom Ross stared down at the sand painting for a moment longer, then finally spat on it.

* * *

That night, after they finished a meager supper of canned pork and beans, Bianchi sang a particularly mournful version of *Barbara Allen* while Tucker unfolded their map and began to inspect it by lantern-light.

'According to this,' he said, 'the mine should be . . . here, near a spot called The Poplars.'

'*If* the map's right,' said Moore.

'Well, the colonel certainly seems to think so. He paid enough for it.'

'But only a fraction of what it's worth,' Moore reminded him. '*If* it's genuine.'

'So it was a good deal.'

Moore glanced over at Bianchi and said: 'Either that or the colonel's been had.'

Tucker chewed on one cheek. The same suspicion had been nagging at him, too. 'I *hope* not,' he said. 'If he has, we'll all pay the price.'

It had been another tough day, but the mood in camp was amiable and relaxed. Their progress had been better than expected, and if the map could be relied on, they could well reach their destination within the next two days.

The campfire burned low. The night was quiet but for the chirping of crickets and the odd scuffle of a salamander rooting among deadfalls for ants and beetles. Moore stifled a yawn. Like Tucker, this was his first real taste of the great outdoors, and he had to confess he was finding it surprisingly agreeable.

Until, that was, a brief but loud wrenching of metal tore the darkness apart.

Everyone sat up and looked around. 'What the hell was that?' asked Tucker.

Ross grabbed up his Winchester twelve-gauge shotgun and quickly pumped in a round. He and Bianchi got up and peered off into the darkness beyond the dying firelight.

'Tom . . . ?' prodded Tucker.

'It came from over there,' said Moore, pointing toward the Studebaker.

Ross exchanged a look with Bianchi and then edged across to the car, which was parked on the other side of the clearing. Bianchi came over, looked Moore in the face, then snatched up the lantern and hurried after him.

As they drew closer to the car they saw that it was rocking gently on its springs, as if someone had just pulled or pushed it. Ross stopped and again searched the night. There was no sound, no movement. Holding the lantern high, Bianchi slowly went around the car.

'*Gesú cristo*,' he whispered when he reached the other side.

'What is it?' called Tucker.

'Somethin's ripped the door off you' car, *signore*.'

'What?'

Tucker hurried around the car to see for himself, while Moore stayed where he was, looking worriedly into the night. Bianchi was right. The door was missing, the hinges bent and buckled where it had been torn free.

'*What?*' Tucker said again.

'Could be a bear,' said Ross, coming to join them. 'Sometimes they get curious, or territorial. Any tracks?'

Bianchi glanced down. 'If there were,'

he said, 'we' messed 'em all up now.'

'Come on,' Ross said. 'We'll build the fire nice and high and that should keep him away.'

'But the car — ' began Tucker, wondering how the hell he was going to explain the damage to the colonel.

'Wait a minute,' said Bianchi. 'He' still out there, Tom. Listen.'

Silence fell. Tucker was about to say he couldn't hear anything when all of a sudden he did. He heard it out there in the darkness, breathing as if through impossibly large lungs . . . whatever *it* was.

Ross quickly brought the shotgun to his shoulder. 'Raise that lantern, Battista,' he said. 'I'll scare the sonofabitch off — '

A branch snapped, loud and clear — on the opposite side of the clearing. Ross spun around, his dark eyes wide. 'Sonofabitch's circlin' us,' he whispered.

They quickly regrouped in the center of the clearing, each man turning slowly as he followed the sounds the bear or whatever it was made creeping through the surrounding shadows. After a while they realized that it wasn't so much circling them as *stalking* them.

'Are you sure it's a bear?' Moore whispered. He was thinking about the sand painting they'd seen earlier, and the fact that Ross had said it was a warning.

Ross aimed the shotgun into the night. 'You'll see the carcass for yourself in just a min — '

Before he could finish the sentence there came a sudden, strange whip of sound and the missing car door spun across the clearing and sheared Tom Ross's head clean off his shoulders.

'*Oh, Christ —* '

'*Jesus, what was —* '

'*Look out!*'

Even as the headless body collapsed, there came a rattling, clicking rush of motion from out of nowhere, and something large and dark snatched Tucker right off his feet. Whatever it was, it kept going, dragging its prey into the rocks with it. Tucker started screaming, and Bianchi accidentally dropped the lantern. It shattered at his feet, plunging them into darkness, and at the same time

Tucker's voice was chopped off in mid-scream.

Moore and Bianchi stood rooted to the spot, not knowing what to do next. Then the heavy rasp of the creature's breathing started growing louder, faster, and they sensed rather than saw another blur of motion through the darkness. All at once something large reared up right behind Moore, jerked him off his feet and snapped his neck —

Crack!

Moore fell dead at its bony feet.

At its bony *paws*.

And knowing that he was going to be next, Battista Bianchi did the only thing he could. He screamed.

3

Jemez Springs nestled between the red rock walls of San Diego Canyon, baking beneath the hard New Mexican sun. From a distance, it looked like just another sprawl of broken-down, mostly single-story adobe buildings that ran along either side of a wide dirt road. Up close it was little better.

On the scrubby flats south of town a plume of yellow dust billowed skyward behind an approaching Model T Ford, but no one noticed the newcomer's imminent arrival. Just then the attention of the townsfolk was elsewhere.

At length the bottle-green Ford entered the outskirts of town and passed the initial few basic dwellings and scrubby cottonwood trees. The first thing that struck the driver was the apparent emptiness of the place. If he hadn't known better, he might have decided that Jemez Springs was a ghost town.

He pulled over and parked in front of a square, adobe-and-timber structure called the Palace Café. He was a tall, lithe-looking man of about six feet, with a strong, clean-shaven jaw and faded green eyes. He looked around. The only witness to his arrival was a violet-green swallow perching on the edge of the café's slanting porch overhang.

The newcomer took off his old sweat-stained campaign hat to reveal short, side-parted hair the color of copper, and then used it to slap dust off his olive cotton shirt and twill canvas pants. He wore the pants tucked into knee-high brown-leather boots, his shirtsleeves rolled back to just above the elbow. His forearms were muscular.

Finally he noticed the ragged crowd gathered around a tall barn or stable that occupied higher ground on the northern edge of town, beside which stood a large, pale khaki safari tent. After a moment he clapped the hat back on and went down to see what was going on.

Odd fragments of conversation carried to him on the warm breeze.

'What happened to the others?'

'Who knows? They can't understand a word he's sayin'.'

At last he reached the fringe of the forty-strong crowd and edged forward to get closer to the barn itself.

Men and women glanced curiously at him as he passed. He had wide shoulders and a broad chest, was in his middle thirties, with a high forehead, a straight nose and a serious manner that missed very little.

At last he reached the barn wall and peered inside through a chink between the board slats. What little sunlight managed to find its way inside turned everything sepia. After a moment his eyes adjusted and he saw about a dozen men surrounding an unlucky thirteenth, who was chained to a peg that had been hammered into the dirt floor. The man was tall and skinny, his curly black hair fanned wildly out from his head, and he was ranting in . . . the words came so fast it took the newcomer a moment to identify it — Italian.

'*Essi sei tutti morti! Essi sei tutti*

morti!' he wailed over and over again.

One of the men surrounding him — short and powerful-looking, with a spill of dirty-fair hair above a rugged, tanned face — made another futile attempt to question him in English. The man on the ground moaned: '*È venuto fuori nulla! Non ho mai visto niente di simile!*'

The newcomer slipped through the press of townsfolk clustered around the door and found himself a space inside the barn, where he sat on a crate. The place smelled of hay, horses, fear and . . . perfume.

Only now did he see that there was a girl among the men surrounding the unfortunate on the ground. She was in her mid twenties, dressed in a blue check shirt and jeans, with a pale, oval face and large gray eyes. She had one arm looped through that of an elderly man who was supporting himself on crutches, his legs being little more than badly twisted stalks.

The fair-haired man kneeling beside the Italian was still trying to question him. 'What-happened?' he asked, speaking slowly and deliberately. 'Bianchi! What-happened? *Capisce?* Tell-me-in-English!'

But the Italian, this Bianchi, kept raving in his own language, saliva frothing at the corners of his mouth. *'Un'ombra! Un'ombra che era venuto da nessuna parte e ucciso tutti! Oh Dio, mi aiuti! Tiene me dal diavolo!'*

The old man on the crutches finally lost patience with the spectacle and turned to face the crowd. 'Does anyone here know what this feller's saying? Anyone outside there?'

There was no answer. The old man glanced around, waiting, hoping. The Italian curled up on the ground at his feet and started crying.

The newcomer finally spoke. 'What happened?' he asked.

All eyes turned toward him. The old cripple squinted through the poor light to see him a little clearer. 'And who're *you?*' he said at length.

'Who wants to know?' countered the newcomer.

The old man drew himself up as best he could. He was a weathered sixty year-old, his eyes the same gray as those of the girl beside him. Once he'd been a powerful man, a man to be reckoned with. Now he was just a shadow of his former self, too thin and too frail to be much use to anyone, and it was clear from his expression that he hated it. As if it should mean something he said: 'I'm Solomon Fogarty. They call me the Colonel.'

'What happened here?' the newcomer asked again.

The answer came from a talkative local standing in the doorway behind him. 'His name's Bianchi,' said the man, his eyes bright with excitement. 'Battista Bianchi. I've known him for years. He staggered into town 'round supper last night, scared out of his wits an' ravin' like a madman . . . '

'And so you pegged him in here like a rabid animal,' said the newcomer, turning to face the colonel again.

'It was for his own safety,' the colonel said. 'We . . . uh . . . figure he spent too long out in the sun, that it turned him crazy.'

'So you worked out what happened to *him*,' said the tall man in the old campaign hat. 'And now you're trying to find out what happened to the others.'

Fogarty bristled. 'What do you know about the others?'

'Only what I heard just now, outside. Plus the fact that this man's trying to tell you that the others — whoever they are — are all dead.'

A collective gasp travelled through the townsfolk crammed into the doorway.

'You speak Eye-talian?' asked the blond man beside the colonel.

'Well enough,' replied the other. 'He says they're all dead. That something came out of the shadows and killed them. That he's never seen anything like it before. And that he wants God to protect him from the Devil.'

The old man eyed him skeptically. 'He's crazy, then, if he's raving about the Devil.' He glanced at the blond man and said: 'Let's clear this place out for a few minutes, Harve.'

The blond nodded and set about shooing the townsfolk out so that he could close the barn doors and give them some small measure of privacy. Everyone left but the colonel, the blond and the girl.

'This here is my daughter, Rachel,' the colonel said gruffly, 'and my assistant surveyor, Harvey Wheeler. You got a name?'

'Jason Hart.'

The colonel used one of his crutches to gesture to the man on the ground. 'Tell him to explain himself,' he said.

Hart knelt beside the Italian. Bianchi was in his early twenties, but his eyes were the eyes of a much older man whose sleep — when he could sleep at all — brought only nightmares.

'*E' il diritto. Tu sei sicuro ora,*' Hart said gently.

Bianchi stared up at him, in no way calmed by the assurance. '*Le ombre!*' he cried desperately. '*L'ombra è venuto a vita e che aveva occhi!*'

Hart put a hand on his arm. '*Credo che lei. Ma tu siete sicuri. Avete capito bene? Tu sei sicuro ora.*' He paused briefly, then asked: '*Si sta dicendo che un'ombra ucciso tutti i vostri amici?'*

'*S-si.'*

'*Dove è successo?'*

'*Su in montagna. Due giorni.'*

'*Grazie.'*

When Hart stood up again the girl demanded to know what he'd said. She was a little more than five and a half feet tall, her auburn hair worn in a loose bob. She had a firm jaw, a determined mouth, a small nose with flared nostrils.

'He said a shadow came and killed everyone,' Hart replied. 'A shadow with eyes.'

Silence but for Bianchi's low mutterings filled the barn. The old man was quick to break it. 'Ridiculous! The man's damn-well mad.'

'Look him in the eyes,' Hart suggested. 'Whatever he saw, he believes it to be the absolute truth. In any case, you won't find any answers with him, colonel. Your answers are two days up on the mountain.'

The colonel's rheumy eyes dropped away from his. 'What do you know about the mountain?' he snapped.

'Nothing,' replied Hart. 'Yet.'

At that moment Bianchi launched himself at Hart and clawed at his shirtfront. 'No, *non hai capito!*' he shrieked. '*Ho visto il diavolo, e il diavolo uccisi tutti!*'

Hart held him by the shoulders and stared directly into his face. After a moment he said with quiet authority: '*Poi mi uccideranno il diavolo.*'

This time the effect of his words was amazing. Bianchi stared at him for a long beat, then finally nodded and allowed some of the tension to drain out of him. He put his head in his hands and started crying again, but this time with relief.

'What did he say?' asked Rachel, frowning.

'He told me he saw the devil. That the devil was going to kill everyone.'

'And you said . . . ?'

'I told him I would just have to kill the devil first.'

Harvey Wheeler took a step forward. 'Just who *are* you, mister?'

'I told you. My name's Hart.'

'He doesn't mean your damn' name!'

the colonel snapped. 'Who *are* you? Where'd you spring from at just this time, and what are you *really* doing here?'

Hart's lips twitched in a brief, grim smile. 'Chasing shadows,' he replied. And to himself he added silently: *Shadows that kill*.

4

After dark a fierce wind sprang up, whirling dust devils along the street. On the slope beside the barn, Colonel Fogarty's safari tent flapped and shivered, and the kerosene lamps hanging from its roof supports made eerie shadows stretch and shrink across the restless canvas.

The colonel himself sat at his small writing desk, tapping one of his crutches against the loose-board floor in a slow, methodical beat. Despite the relative comfort of their surroundings — well-stuffed fireside chairs set around a portable Reznor Company oil heater, a wind-up gramophone, a scattering of colorful Afghan rugs — Rachel seemed equally uneasy. This time yesterday everything had been going to plan. They were expecting Tucker and Moore to return within five days and over dinner the colonel had told her they'd better start hiring men and ordering equipment up from Albuquerque.

'It's already taken care of,' she'd replied.

Her father had stopped with his fork halfway to his lips, and stared at her. 'Could I have taught my child a little *too* well?' he'd asked playfully.

'Could you *ever* teach your child too well?' she'd countered, and in that moment there had been a connection between them, a bond that hadn't always been there but was now infinitely sweet.

The colonel had always been a man of action, and he'd never made any secret of his disappointment when his wife had died in the act of giving him a daughter instead of a son. That was why Rachel had worked so hard to win his approval.

Not that it had been easy. The colonel's life had always been one of travel, quest and conquest, and he was rarely at home during her formative years. He'd spent most of his life speculating in a variety of enterprises, everything from previously unheard-of service stations to discount food stores, and because Congress had made dealing with the Patent Office so slow and difficult, he'd made even more money backing promising inventions and smoothing the way for their registration. In 1916, without a word to anyone, he had enlisted in the Georgia National Guard and travelled down to Mexico to lock horns with the radical, Pancho Villa.

Only after he'd lost the use of his legs did Rachel get the chance to truly prove her worth to him. Now he was as devoted to her as she was to him.

Their latest enterprise had been set to reap the greatest reward yet, and set her up for life.

On his travels the colonel had learned of a map that led to a potential fortune in ores and minerals up in the Jemez Mountains, and had become obsessed with tracking it down. He'd hired a private detective to do just that, and eventually traced it to a recluse named Saxon, who lived in Brawley, Arizona. When asked why he had chosen to sit on the map instead of exploit it, Saxon had been vague. He'd run into problems on the mountain, he'd said, and come so close to dying that his nerve had broken and he'd returned to Brawley as the colonel saw him now — a shell of his former self.

Exploiting the man's obvious frailty, Colonel Fogarty had offered a pitifully small amount for the map, willing to let the other man bid him up. But to his surprise Saxon had accepted his first offer. He hadn't thought much about it at the time, but now, in light of Bianchi's ravings, he began to suspect that Saxon had just been glad to be rid of the thing.

Almost as soon as the thought occurred to him the colonel dismissed it as nonsense. Still, he couldn't deny that this entire enterprise was a tremendous gamble. The map had a dubious provenance at best. If it proved to be worthless, then they stood to lose a sizeable chunk of their wealth. But if it paid off . . .

Of course, nothing could have prepared them for what had happened to Tucker, Moore and the man Ross. How could they have expected such a turn of events? But right now they had other, more pressing concerns.

'If a panic starts, we've got a financial disaster in our laps,' the old man said at last. 'If our investors get word of this, we could lose damn'-near everything.'

Rachel stopped her pacing, glad that he had finally raised the subject that was in both their minds. 'Father,' she said hesitantly.

He turned in his little ash-and-canvas camp chair and eyed her expectantly.

'What do you suppose *could* be up there?' she asked.

He made an irritable gesture. 'Nothing more than a madman's tale told to a herd of sheep.'

'But what if it isn't? It has to be *something*. And whatever it was, it unhinged the Italian.'

'Of course it's *something*,' he agreed. 'But the *Devil?* A shadow with eyes? Come *on*, now, Rae. More likely it's the work of Indians or bandits or a torn-up bear or mountain lion.'

The wind had dropped during their exchange, but the respite from its mournful howl was only temporary. All at once it seemed to gather itself and batter the tent with one gust that was stronger than the rest. The tent top snapped and rippled, and their shadows stretched and contorted as if panicking at the sound.

As it dropped again there came an odd resonance from some dark corner of the wilderness near town. They both heard it. It sounded like someone playing a flute. Rachel paused again, eyed her father carefully, then went across to the tent flap and pushed it aside.

From here she had a good view of the moon-silvered street below. Dust spiraled everywhere, stinging her skin and making her wince. About midway along the street a single lantern hanging from a pole tilted oddly, and for just a moment, within its light, something moved and then was gone.

Rachel had just convinced herself that it was some sort of trick when she spotted another stir of movement.

This time she caught her breath.

An old Indian shuffled out of the shadows and headed down toward the café. He was short and stocky, dressed in an ancient army frockcoat, the front of which glistened with a jumble of tarnished medals. He walked on warped legs, and his long hair, the color of smoke, whipped wildly around a wrinkled face that was the color of an old, old penny. He carried a thin, blackened length of wood tucked behind his belt, about three feet long.

She closed the tent flap and stood quietly for a moment, thinking. Behind her, the colonel said: 'Don't tell me you're worried it's — '

She turned and gave him a look that silenced him. 'I'm worried just like you're worried,' she said firmly. 'That we've invested heavily in this project and that I'm damned if we're going to lose our money for the sake of a fairy tale.'

The colonel nodded, admiring her tenacity. 'Is that man's automobile still parked outside the café?'

'Yes.'

'Who is he?' he wondered softly. 'He comes to town this morning, right out of nowhere. He gives us a name that might be false and offers us some guff about chasing shadows that's little more than a riddle. How do we know he was telling us what Bianchi *really* said?'

Rachel considered that for a short moment. 'Maybe he wants us out of those mountains. Maybe he's done some mining himself. There's a world of maybes with someone like that, father.'

'And yet my water tells me he's honest.'

'Perhaps. But *how* honest?'

'Only time'll tell that,' the colonel said. 'Either way we have problems that have to be solved before our men get here.'

Again the wind tore at the walls of the tent. She looked back at the tent flap, where wind-driven dust drifted inside. 'Hart's right about one thing, though,' she said. 'The answer to whatever happened out there *is* two days up on the mountain.'

He nodded and, reaching a decision, pushed awkwardly to his feet. 'Yes. And that being the case, we're going to have to send a search party up there to discover what it is.'

5

There were no bars in Jemez Springs, of course. Prohibition had seen to that. So the focal point of town was the Palace Café, where locals tended to gather and socialize in the evenings and — officially — drink nothing stronger than coffee.

Tonight was no different. The café was a square building of medium size, the roof low with old wooden beams, the stucco walls painted white. A curtained doorway behind the counter led to the kitchen out back. About a dozen tables occupied the main room, and a small upright piano stood incongruously in one shadowed corner.

The windows had been shuttered but still the lanterns strung from the ceiling swayed back and forth, pushed by stray draughts. The shutters themselves rattled and banged, adding to the already-uneasy atmosphere.

Most of the men present were still

talking about what had happened to Bianchi and the others. Speculation was as wild as it was rife.

Jason Hart sat alone at a corner table, writing neatly in a small, leather-bound journal. A selection of pamphlets was fanned out on the table beside him. Every so often he stopped writing to consult one.

The door to the bar opened and the wind blew in a whirl of dust. The old Indian — Bidziil, though no one here knew him — let himself in. He stood there for a moment, surveying the room, until a huge man with a full black beard yelled: 'Close that door, you damn' fool!'

Bidziil closed the door, but in his own sweet time. Then he went up to the counter, past Harvey Wheeler, who was studying Hart thoughtfully over the lip of his moonshine-laced cup of coffee. The old shaman ordered coffee, black. He seemed unaware of the scrutiny he was receiving from the big man who'd told him to close the door, and the big man's companion, a smaller, more wiry individual in a dented derby hat.

As Bidziil put some coins down on the counter, the big man leaned forward and peered closely at his profile. 'Come to admire your handiwork, have you?' he growled.

Bidziil glanced at him, then turned his attention to the cup the café-owner pushed across the counter at him.

'Why don't you go on up to the barn on the hill?' the big man continued. He was so big he looked as if he'd been built out of girders. 'He's still in there, you know, chained to the ground. The poor bastard you and the rest of your heathen brothers scared half to death.'

The café-owner eyed him nervously. 'Let it go, Corrigan,' he said.

The man named Corrigan ignored him. He was dressed in a long buckskin coat and jeans, and beneath his long, matted beard his face was well-worn, that of a forty year-old who looked half again that age.

'You heard me, old man,' Corrigan went on. 'What the hell have your people been doing up there?'

At first Bidziil ignored him. Then,

aware that he had become the focus of attention, he finally allowed himself a faint twitch of leathery lips. As he looked again at Corrigan his expression clearly said: *Wouldn't you like to know?*

Corrigan grimaced, unsettled by Bidziil's calm refusal to be intimidated. 'You old fool,' he continued, albeit with a sudden, curious lack of conviction. 'I ought to chop your hands off and strangle you with 'em.'

'He's nothing,' said the owner of the café, anxious to avoid trouble. 'Leave him be.'

Bidziil took his coffee and looked around for a place to sit. The other patrons pointedly turned their backs on him. At last his near-black eyes settled on a single empty table in the middle of the room, from which all the chairs had been taken. He looked around some more, but no one offered him a spare chair.

Then Hart pressed his boot against one of the empty chairs on the other side of his table and slid it out toward the Indian. The sound it made moving across the floorboards was loud and laddery in the uneasy silence. The Indian weaved between tables, took the chair, nodded his thanks and then went to sit alone in the center of the room.

At last conversation picked up again and Hart went back to writing until a shadow fell across the page. When he looked up, he saw Harvey Wheeler tilting his head so that he could read the title of one of the pamphlets on the table before him. It read:

THE LONDON SOCIETY FOR PSYCHICAL RESEARCH

A PAMPHLET on Psychical Phenomena, Ectoplasmic and Poltergeist Activities
By
William Henry Myers

'If you don't mind,' Hart said mildly, 'you're blocking my light.'

Wheeler's hazel eyes moved slowly to his face. 'Is that a fact?'

'Did you want something?'

Wheeler nodded. 'Now that you mention it — '

But before the surveyor could say more, the door opened again and dust spiraled inside ahead of the colonel and his daughter, who was carrying a small leather satchel over one shoulder.

Bundled against the sharp night wind in a gray crushed velvet jacket, Rachel immediately spotted Wheeler standing over Hart's table as she closed the door behind her. When she looked at Hart, Wheeler saw something in her face that he didn't like.

The colonel, meanwhile, hobbled to the counter, where he finally turned back to face the room. When he was sure he had their attention he said: 'Men, let's have a little powwow here.'

Once again silence descended over the café. Rachel set her satchel down on the counter and began to set out five stacks of twenty-dollar gold pieces.

'I've come quite a few miles in my life,' the colonel continued. 'I mined diamonds in Africa before most of you were born. When I was in Bolivia, at Potosi, we had to fight natives and mosquitoes every inch of the way. I lost the use of my legs in

Kentucky. Ten days below ground in the pitch black. Not that I'm grumbling. Every glory hole has its hell getting to it. If it was easy, well . . . the price of *easy* is two cents on the dollar.'

All eyes were fixed on Rachel, as she quietly and meticulously set out the double-eagles.

'Now, I know you've all heard the rumors about what happened — what we've been *told* happened — up in the mountains. And I'm equally sure we're all old enough and sensible enough to know that the boogeyman was just something our parents thought up to scare us when we were kids. I don't believe for one moment that my men met their ends up there by anything other than natural means, but I need someone to go find out just what those natural means were. So who'll be the first to go clear this trifle up?'

He looked expectantly around the room, his eyes moving across Corrigan and his small, thin-faced companion, before finally coming to rest on Hart.

'Come on now,' he said persuasively.

'Don't be shy. I need five men, one for each of those hundred-dollar stacks my daughter's putting out right now. Any man who steps forward gets a hundred dollars up front for going and the same again when he gets back. But I need a good man for each stack.'

Once again he scanned the room. Rachel's eyes found those of Hart. The silence was heavy.

'Are we listening to madmen now?' demanded the colonel. 'Is that the way it is? You've heard all that nonsense spouted by Bianchi and you actually *believe* it?'

But if he was hoping to shame his audience into accepting his offer, he was to be disappointed. Silence continued to reign.

'By God, if I could drag myself up there I'd disgrace the lot of you,' he said, disgusted.

That got a reaction, for no man takes kindly to being called a coward. From somewhere at the back of the room a voice demanded: 'If it's no big deal, why don't you send your daughter?'

The colonel moved as quickly as he

could to seek out the speaker. 'I should whip you just for the thought of it,' he rasped. 'You really think I'd send a woman to do what you're too *afraid* to do?'

The men started muttering darkly among themselves. Rachel faced them all square on for a long moment, then turned around and scooped a stack of double eagles off the bar.

'All right,' she said loudly. 'I'll be the first.'

A shockwave passed through the room, restoring the silence.

Rattled, the colonel said: 'Now, listen here . . . '

Ignoring him, she faced the others again and demanded: 'Well? Who'll come with me?'

At first there was no reaction.

And then, abruptly, Corrigan came over, took off his dark slouch hat and swept one stack into it, then a second. 'Me an' Harmonica Jones'll bookend you, ma'am,' he said, hooking a thumb at his skinny partner.

'Hey, now . . . ' grumbled Harmonica,

pushing away from the counter.

Rachel turned her attention back to Hart, but her words were addressed to the room at large. 'Are these two the only real men here?'

Harvey Wheeler reacted. He clumped back across the floor, took his stack of double eagles from the bar, then grabbed Rachel's small right hand and dumped them into it.

'I'll go for nothing,' he said quietly.

But she wasn't having that. She took the money and slapped it back into his hand, and he knew better than to argue with her. 'Father,' she said, 'four will do.'

The colonel nodded grimly, then turned his back on their audience and barked: 'Coffee! *Now!*'

6

As things started getting back to normal, Harmonica Jones scowled at Dan Corrigan and hissed: 'What the hell are you doing? You heard the rumors — '

'Rumors,' said Corrigan, grinning down at him. 'That's all they are. Anyway, you got nothing to worry about. I'll watch your back while we're up there. Would you do the same for me?'

'I wouldn't let you down, if that's what you mean.'

'But if it was to come to it, you know, something happened. Is there anyone else you'd sooner have looking out for you?'

'No,' Harmonica said. 'And you know it.'

'Then wipe that worried look off your face, pard. The colonel's a powerful man. We impress him, prove our worth, we'll be sitting pretty.'

Harmonica narrowed watery blue eyes at him. 'What's going on in that sneaky

47

brain of yours?' he asked, low-voiced.

'That's for me to know — for the time being,' Corrigan replied in sudden good humor. 'Let's just say I've got a game playing out in my head, Harmonica. I certainly do.'

★ ★ ★

Hart, meanwhile, was just about to go back to his journal when Rachel came over and sat down across from him without waiting to be invited. He closed his journal and returned her level stare for several moments.

'Yes, ma'am?' he finally asked.

'The money didn't tempt you?'

'I don't need the money, Miss Fogarty.'

'Everyone needs money.'

'Then let's put it this way. I already have a job. I don't need another one.'

'Then what *do* you need, Mr Hart?'

'I'm not sure I under — '

'Why *are* you here?' she prodded. And then, after the briefest hesitation: 'The mining?'

'No, ma'am.'

'Well, if it isn't the mining and it's not money, what *is* it?'

'Curiosity,' he replied.

'About . . . ?'

'What's up on that mountain. Or what *isn't.*'

'I don't follow.'

'It's simple enough,' he said. 'Whatever killed three of your men could just as easily have killed the fourth. It didn't. It allowed him to come back here, to Jemez Springs, and after a fashion tell you people what had happened up there. You get it now, Miss Fogarty? It was sending you a warning, telling you to leave those mountains alone.'

'And you want to know why.'

'Yes, ma'am, I do.'

'And what business is that of yours, Mr Hart?'

He was about to tell her when the wind picked up again and one of the shutters slammed open. A fierce gust of wind rushed in and blew out all the lanterns, throwing the room into darkness.

At once there was uproar, followed by hurried footsteps as men got up and searched themselves for matches in order to get the lamps working again. The wind howled along the wide street and around the small café. A silhouette appeared at the window and slammed the shutter closed. But still the wailing went on, and one by one they realized that the sound was actually coming from inside the café itself.

A match sizzled to life. Hart got the nearest lantern working again and a dull amber glow quickly bled back into the room, sending the shadows running.

Bidziil was standing in the middle of the floor, and it was he who was making the horrifying dirge.

Everyone reared back and watched him warily. Unaware of his audience he kept chanting, his eyes tight shut, his head tilted up toward the still-shadowy ceiling.

A moment later the old Indian stabbed a finger at the table, upon which he had used a stub of chalk to draw four stick figures, three of whom had their heads lopped off.

Bug-eyed, and knowing that one of those figures was meant to represent him,

Corrigan growled and dragged a .38-caliber Colt Army Special from his waistband. Men immediately scrambled out of the way but the old Indian stood his ground, even when Corrigan took aim and blew a ragged hole through the tabletop.

Smoke filled the room and coiled lazily toward the ceiling. Still the Indian continued to wail and chant. Jaw tight, Corrigan stalked across to him, placed the warm muzzle against the Indian's forehead and thumbed back the hammer.

When they spoke about it later, no one actually remembered seeing Hart move. One moment he was standing beside the lantern he'd just lit, the next he was simply *there,* shoving Corrigan's gun-hand toward the ceiling even as Corrigan himself pulled the trigger.

The gun exploded with a roar and a flash, and the load punched a deceptively small hole in the ceiling.

Then Corrigan wrenched his gun back and spun toward Hart. As he made to throw a punch, the spell holding their audience finally broke. They grabbed Corrigan and dragged him back, while the café-owner moved quickly to hustle Bidziil toward the door and out into the night.

Corrigan's dark eyes glittered as they burned into Hart's face. 'It's a real pity what you just did, feller,' he snarled.

'I thought you'd see it that way,' Hart said.

'Don't think this ends here!' yelled Corrigan as his captors turned him away. 'I'm long on memory, boy!'

'But short on sight,' Hart replied mildly.

He followed the café-owner to the door and looked out into the wild night. Bidziil was standing in the middle of the street, still chanting, his words whipped away by the wind, which abruptly grew fiercer still.

Dust began to spiral higher, making it more difficult to see the Indian. Hart narrowed his eyes, sure that something was happening to the man, that he was . . . *changing* somehow . . .

And then the wind died down and the street was empty, the Indian nowhere to be seen.

7

The following morning the little expedition prepared to leave town. Under Harvey Wheeler's watchful eye Corrigan and Harmonica loaded supplies aboard a four year-old Ford Model T pickup, while Rachel, her jeans tucked into sturdy brown boots, walked up to the tent beside the barn and said goodbye to her father.

In the light of a new day, the colonel looked older than usual, and more uneasy than ever with his daughter's decision to go up into the hills. Still, he knew better than to argue with her. Rachel was too much like him. And once *his* mind was made up . . .

They looked at each other wordlessly for a while, and then Rachel hugged the old man and rubbed him warmly between the shoulders. When they finally broke apart she said: 'I'll see you in a few days.'

He didn't appear to have heard her. He was staring off toward the distant, misty vastness of the mountains. 'If only I could go instead of you,' he murmured.

'You'll never change,' she said fondly. 'Always hankering after adventure.'

He summoned a faint smile. 'I love you, daughter.'

'And I love *you*, father.'

Wheeler strode briskly up the slope, breaking the moment. 'We're ready,' he called.

Rachel turned and nodded, then gave her father one final kiss and brushed past Wheeler and down toward the pickup. The surveyor turned and watched her go.

'Watch her close,' the colonel instructed. 'If anything happens to her, you'll answer to me.'

'I'll keep her safe,' Wheeler promised.

A few minutes later the pickup sputtered to life, a belch of smoke burst from the exhaust. Then it was rattling out of Jemez Springs, and Colonel Fogarty was left to lean on his crutches and watch the thin cloud of dust it raised heading toward the far-off mountains.

★   ★   ★

The hills shelved skyward, their deep mustard-yellow bulk showing stark against the brassy blue, and the day was quick to heat up. Progress was slow, but by the middle of the afternoon they were well into the foothills. They had to stop shortly thereafter, when the pickup threatened to overheat, and while they gave it a chance to cool off, Corrigan and Harmonica slumped into shade and drank from their canteens.

Wheeler stared at Rachel as Rachel walked back along the trail and peered down the mountain, one hand shielding her eyes from the afternoon glare. Jemez Springs was barely visible now, all but lost in the gelatinous shimmer of over-hot air. After a while the surveyor called: 'He's not coming.'

She turned to face him.' What was that?'

'I said he's not coming.'

'Who?'

'Hart. He left this morning. Before dawn.'

She came closer. 'What makes you think I was looking for him?'

He shrugged. 'It didn't take much

working out. I saw the way you were looking at him yesterday.'

'Oh? And how was that?'

'Like you were about an inch away from throwing yourself at him.'

She bristled but held her temper. She didn't want to make a scene in front of Corrigan and his skinny companion. 'Let's get something straight, Harvey,' she said quietly. 'I'm the boss's daughter. You're the hired hand. Do me a favor and try not to forget it.'

He only grinned. 'When you're not quite so angry you might feel differently about me.'

She eyed him coolly. 'We've been through all this before, Harve. I'd never involve myself with a man like you. *Never.* God, if it was up to me I wouldn't even have you here *now.*'

'You may need me before this is through,' he reminded her.

It was on the tip of her tongue to tell him that was hardly likely. But even as she went to say it the words died in her throat, because it suddenly occurred to her that, given what had happened to

56

Tucker, Moore and Tom Ross, he might very well be right.

★ ★ ★

They pushed on through what was left of the afternoon. The sun began a slow slide toward dusk. Around them, the mountains swallowed all sound and conjured an unsettling sense of isolation and claustrophobia.

In back of the pickup, Corrigan was deep in thought, while Harmonica played a mournful tune on the instrument for which he'd earned his nickname.

'How come you're so quiet?' Harmonica asked after a while.

Corrigan grinned through the thick tangle of his beard. 'I'm planning how to be a mine owner,' he replied cryptically.

★ ★ ★

Corrigan spotted the vultures early the following morning and pointed one fat, thick finger in their direction. 'Them yellow heads say we ain't far now.'

The night had been long and, for Rachel at least, even more disquieting than she could have imagined. As the sun went down it had thrown long shadows across the seemingly empty land and dyed the sky the color of blood. And as night fell with a totality that even their lanterns seemed unable to relieve, so too came the silence. The mountains seemed almost to hiss with it.

The temperature had plunged, the day's enervating heat becoming just a memory, and Rachel found it easy to believe that what Bianchi had told them was true — that shadows up here *could* come to life and kill the people they didn't turn crazy. It was a thought that kept her awake long into the after-midnight hours.

Now she followed Corrigan's pointing finger and knew that the vultures could mean nothing good.

Less than an hour later they came around a long turn in the rocks and she spotted the sand painting up ahead. At her command Wheeler braked and she jumped out to get a closer look at it.

Leaving the engine idling, Wheeler and the others hurried to join her.

For a moment they just stood there, trying to make sense of it. By any stretch it was a work of art, albeit a troubling one.

'What the heck *is* that?' asked Harmonica.

Corrigan stated the obvious. 'Some kinda sand painting.'

'I know that. I mean, what's it supposed to represent? And what's it doing out here in the middle of nowhere?'

As he thoughtfully traced the half-man, half-beast in the center of the wheel lines, a miniature landslide of gravel came skittering down the slope.

As one they leapt back and quickly checked their surroundings. There was no movement now that the last of the gravel had slid to a halt. But Rachel for one had the unshakable sense of being watched.

'You're letting your imaginations run away with you,' Wheeler said.

Corrigan nodded, keeping his eyes on the ridge. 'I guess. There's nothing up th — '

The pickup's engine suddenly cut out.

Another ominous silence filled the high country in its wake. Everyone exchanged looks, and then Wheeler stalked back to the pickup, dragged the S-shaped starter handle from under the driver's seat and jabbed it in Corrigan's direction. Corrigan took it, went around and inserted it into the front of the pickup and gave it a turn.

Nothing happened, except that another miniature landslide slithered down the slope behind them.

'Try it again,' Wheeler called. 'And watch yourself. Sometimes it kicks back.'

Corrigan gave the starter handle another turn. This time the pickup's engine made a sick-sounding whir and cough.

More gravel bounced and rolled down the slope. Rachel lifted one hand to shield her eyes from the sun and scoured the ridge. Nothing.

Behind her the engine suddenly spluttered to life, and Wheeler busied himself retarding the spark and working the throttle. 'Come on!' he called. 'We've wasted enough time out here!'

They climbed back aboard the truck. Wheeler released the brake and sent them back on their way. Behind them the land fell quiet and still.

Then another miniature landslide of gravel trickled slowly down the slope.

★   ★   ★

Shortly before sundown they made a sharp right turn and came out onto a shelf of land that would make a good campsite for the coming evening.

Trouble was, someone had already beaten them to it.

Wheeler recognized Jason Hart's bottle-green Model T immediately, and stamped on the brake. Hart himself was hunkered beside a small fire, watching them over the rim of his enamel coffee cup.

Rachel, secretly heartened to see him though she had no true idea why, opened her door, hopped down and strode across to him. Behind her, Wheeler fairly threw himself out of the cab with his fists bunched. Corrigan jumped down and

61

hurried after him, Harmonica not far behind.

Hart rose to his feet and watched them come. As she drew nearer, Rachel thought he looked curiously older than he had back in town. It came to her that perhaps what he'd seen up here had aged him, and the thought made her shiver.

'What are you up doing here?' she demanded.

Hart ran green eyes across each of them in turn, then said softly: 'I wanted to see those men and where they died before you turned up and disturbed everything.'

Wheeler frowned, not really understanding the answer.

'And have you?' asked Rachel.

He nodded.

'Do you know what killed them?'

'Yes,' he replied. 'But I doubt that you'll believe me, even if I tell you.'

8

Rachel, Wheeler, Corrigan and Harmonica glanced at each other. The atmosphere suddenly became even more disquieting.

Corrigan was the first to find his voice again. 'Why don't you try us?'

Hart held back a moment before saying: 'Did you happen to notice a sand painting back along the trail? You'd have come across it sometime this morning.'

Harmonica nodded. 'Yeah. It was a ratty-looking wolf-thing.'

'In Navaho it's called *yee nadlooshii*, which means to walk or travel like an animal. We'd call it a shape-shifter — and I think the Navaho have called one up.'

For another moment there was only stunned silence. Then Wheeler made an impatient scoffing sound. 'In other words, you don't know *squat*.'

But Hart seemed so sincere about it that Rachel at least was willing to hear him out. 'What exactly is a shape-shifter?' she asked.

'A being that has the power to transform itself into an animal,' he replied. 'A wolf, say, or a crow, a fox or an owl. I recognize this one. He's called Maii'.'

'You don't believe that,' she said.

'You asked me what killed them, Miss Fogarty. I've told you. Maii' — Coyote — is an important figure in Navajo belief. He's one of the few aspects of Navajo life that isn't riddled with taboo and superstition. He's a god, a trickster, an evil spirit, always there, lurking just out of sight. He's immortal, he can't be killed. The Navajo also say something else about him — that if Coyote crosses your path, turn back and don't continue your journey. If you do, something bad will happen to you. You'll be hurt, or killed.'

'The Irish say much the same thing,' growled Corrigan. 'But they say it only happens if you meet a red-haired woman.'

'Whatever killed those men and turned Bianchi into a raving lunatic was more than just some fairy-tale monster,' said Wheeler. 'He was flesh and blood, and

I'm going to find him and make him pay for it!'

He nodded at Corrigan, and Corrigan suddenly produced his .38 and pointed it at Hart. 'No sudden moves, mister!'

Rachel's mouth dropped open in shock. 'What do you think you're doing?'

It was Wheeler who replied. 'I want to know who this man is and what he's *really* doing up here.'

'*What?*'

'For all we know, the Indians paid him to help run us off,' said Wheeler. 'It could even be that he killed our men himself.'

'I don't think even a fool like you believes *that*,' Hart said mildly.

'So convince me otherwise. Who are you, really?'

'My name is Jason Hart.'

'Why are you here?'

'I told you. I wanted to find out what was up here. What killed your men.'

'Again — *why?* What business is it of yours? And don't give me that guff about chasing shadows.'

'Then let's just say I'm a searcher,' said Hart. 'I go after the truth.'

Wheeler's top lip curled. 'You're not gonna give me a single straight answer, are you?' he said, and before Hart could stop him, he snatched up the satchel that had been resting against the Ford.

He tore it open and upended its contents onto the hot sand, but nothing there gave him the answers he sought, either. There was a journal, a small wooden box, two books, one on science, the other on the nature of death. Wheeler opened the wooden box, found only a selection of medical instruments.

'All right,' he breathed. 'We'll see what you're hiding in your *car!*'

Rachel could only watch as he opened the trunk and rummaged inside. He scooped books out onto the ground, unearthed a microscope, spilled a selection of pamphlets.

Hart watched stoically.

Rachel went over to the car and picked up some of the pamphlets. She saw names like Dr Hodgson and Professor Hyslop, Reverend Stainton Moses, Mrs Sedgwick, William Myers and Edmond Gurney.

Then she noticed the edge of a letter protruding from one of the pamphlets, and drew it out. The letterhead identified it as having come from *The London Society for Psychical Research*. The body of the letter complimented Hart on his 'enlightening investigations' into something called 'the Mesmer trance.' It was signed by William Myers.

Rachel folded the letter and slipped it back into the pamphlet. Reaching a decision, she turned and said: 'Corrigan! Put the gun down.'

The big man hesitated, his eyes moving to Wheeler.

'I said put it down,' she repeated more firmly. 'And Harvey — leave his stuff alone.'

But Wheeler, determined to find something to confirm his suspicions, kept searching. Rachel turned to Corrigan and said: 'Mr. Corrigan, since you now work for me, I'm ordering you to shoot Mr. Wheeler if doesn't stop right this minute!'

For an instant Wheeler froze, then turned to see if she was bluffing. One look at the suddenly-hard planes of her face told him she wasn't.

'Are you crazy?' he asked.

'No,' she replied. 'But sometimes I think *you* are.'

He saw then that any hope he'd ever had of winning this woman over, any chance he'd had of marrying into the Fogarty dynasty, had vanished.

His mood abruptly grew darker still.

Temporarily lost for words, he shook his head at her. But finally he backed off and glared at Hart. 'You've seen them, then,' he said. 'Tucker, Moore and Ross. The dead men.'

Hart nodded, and setting his cup aside started to pick up his scattered belongings.

'How did they die?'

'Horribly,' he replied without looking up.

'Far from here?'

'A mile or so.'

'So you nosed around, looked at the bodies. Did you find any tracks?'

'A few. Animal tracks. A *large* animal.'

'A bear?'

'Not a bear, no. Whatever it was, it was

larger than that.'

'You're lying,' Wheeler said.

He went to knock the books out of Hart's hand, but Hart moved faster. With swift efficiency he caught Wheeler's wrist in his free hand and twisted. Instantly Wheeler fell to his knees, his face a mask of pain. He struggled to break the hold but it was useless. Hart's grip was like that of a vise.

Rachel quickly moved between them. 'That's *enough!*' she snapped. 'It's over, and I can only apologize for what Harvey did to your belongings.'

'Apology accepted,' Hart replied. Then, to Wheeler: 'But don't *ever* touch my things again.'

He released Wheeler's wrist.

'That's better,' said Rachel. She backed off, pulled down a breath and struggled to compose herself. 'All right,' she continued at last. 'It's too late to press on now, so we'll make camp here, as we planned, and then move on again first thing tomorrow. And *you*, Mr Hart . . . '

'Yes, ma'am?'

'You'll come with us, take us to the

spot where our men died. I don't believe what Harvey had to say about you working with the Indians or committing murder, but I *do* know I'll be happier having you where I can keep my eye on you.'

He only nodded.

9

Night dropped like a cold blanket. The newcomers made camp, raised tents, fixed supper and ate in silence, and then Harmonica took out his mouth organ and started to play softly. Hart kept to himself until Rachel came over and asked if she could join him.

'Help yourself,' he said.

She sat across the small fire from him, asking: 'What will **we** find ahead of us tomorrow?'

'Graves,' he said.

'You buried them? Our men?'

'It seemed like the decent thing to do. You can always take them back yourselves or send someone up to reclaim them, if they have families.'

'Thank you . . . ' She was quiet for a while, then she said: 'I really don't know what to make of you, Mr Hart. You seem genuine, and yet some of the things you say, about shape-shifters and such . . . '

'You find it hard to believe.'

'Well, you must admit, it does sound pretty outlandish.' She smiled to take some of the sting out of her words. 'How exactly did you come to start 'chasing shadows' for a living, anyway?'

He thought about it for a moment. 'I guess it was all down to my grand-mother. She came to live with us when she got too old to really take care of herself and I grew very close to her. She used to come into my room every night and sit on the edge of the bed and tell me fairy stories till I drifted off to sleep. I never knew anyone who could tell a story better.

'Then, one night, she came in and sat on the edge of the bed and started telling me about . . . other things. Another life, beyond this one. She told me that this life was really just a proving ground, a chance for us to face one choice after another and always do the right thing so that we could grow and learn and prove our worth to . . . I don't know, some higher power, I guess.

'The more she told me, the more I

realized that it's true what they say — that we really don't know what we don't know yet. There's so much more out there, beyond the veil, things we could never even imagine. And so I resolved to discover and understand as much of those seldom-seen things as I could.'

She pondered that, and then asked: 'Did it never occur to you that your grandmother might have been wrong about all that? That we just live, then die, and that's all there is to it?'

'No, Miss Fogarty,' he replied. 'Because the night I'm talking about, the night she came in and told me all those things . . . it was two weeks after she'd passed away and a week after her funeral.'

A shiver trickled down her spine. 'Are you telling me you saw her *ghost?*'

'I guess I am.'

She looked at his face in the fire-glow, searching for something that would tell her he was joking or lying. But saw only the truth, as he believed it.

'It could just as well have been your imagination,' she argued. 'You were only young, after all.'

'Of course. That's why I decided to devote my life to finding out one way or the other.'

'And what conclusion have you reached so far?'

'Only that the light of reason often throws up more questions than it answers.'

'In other words,' she said, 'nothing.'

'I wouldn't say that.' He glanced off to his left and indicated the rock wall behind them with a nod. 'Let's just imagine for a moment that we don't have a fire burning, or the light from our lanterns. What would you see over there?'

'Nothing. Just darkness.'

'And if we were to light a lantern?'

'It would chase the darkness away, and we'd see the rocks.'

'Anything else?' he asked.

She thought for a moment, then said: 'Shadows. We'd see new shadows. Shadows that weren't there before.'

He smiled at her. 'There's hope for you yet, Miss Fogarty,' he said. 'And that's what happens when we shine the light of reason on something. We reveal a little of it, of its *truth*, but that light also casts shadows on the rest.'

'And that's where you go?'

He nodded. 'Where the shadows are darkest.'

She shivered.

'What about you?' he asked suddenly. 'Why are you so interested in this place?'

She saw no reason to evade the question. 'My father bought a map. If it's accurate, it will take us to a lost mine, and potentially a fortune in ores and minerals.'

'This?' he asked, taking a photostatic copy of the colonel's map out of his back pocket and handing it over. It was creased and very faintly bloodstained. 'I took it from one of your men. He was still holding it when he died.'

She swallowed softly as she unfolded the map and nodded. 'That's it.'

'So,' he said. 'You plan to tear the mountains open and plunder them of their riches.'

'I prefer to call it developing the area's potential,' she said stiffly.

'I'm only telling you how the Indians

must see it. Trying to understand just why they summoned a shape-shifter to stop you.'

She cocked her head at him. 'You really believe this, don't you?'

'Uh-huh. I've spent practically my whole life studying phenomena like this. I know such creatures exist. I know it's possible to call them up.'

'But do you have any real proof?'

'Mythology is filled with accounts of shape-shifters. Zeus is said to have changed shape so that he could seduce mortal women. On one occasion he turned himself into a swan in order to beguile Leda, wife of the Spartan leader Tyndareus. To satisfy his lust for the Phoenician nymph Europa, he turned himself into a bull. Some Norse warriors were said to change into wolves and bears in order to fight more effectively.'

'But that's just mythology. You said so yourself. What real proof do you have?'

'I saw what it did to your men.'

'That would hardly stand up in a court of law.'

'Then all I can ask is that you keep an open mind, Miss Fogarty, and take extra care until this little expedition is over and we're all back in Jemez Springs.'

'Mr Hart,' she said, 'you're starting to scare me. And I don't scare easy.'

'Then take that extra care. Myth has it that a shape-shifter can invade your mind. Turn you around. That they eat human flesh and sleep with the dead.'

'I'll tell you what we're dealing with,' called Wheeler. 'Straw men, nothing more, nothing less. Those digger Indians are calling up the bottom of the rotgut barrel with a little paint and dirt to try and scare us off.'

'The men I buried earlier today tell a different story,' Hart said. 'And so does Bianchi.'

'Well,' said Rachel. 'If I have night-mares tonight — assuming I get any sleep at all, that is — I know I'll have you to blame, Mr Hart.'

'Call me Jase,' he said.

She looked down at him for a moment, then smiled. He was right, of course — there was no point in standing on ceremony if they were going to be travelling together. 'All right — Jase it is,' she said. 'And you may call me Rae.'

'Goodnight, Rae,' he said. 'Sleep well.'

10

They got an early start the following morning. Hart led the way and, acting on impulse, Rachel decided to accompany him in his Ford — a decision that did little to endear either of them to Wheeler.

The land was all-enveloping, with great basalt cliffs rising behind massive stands of pine and fir. Rachel, mentally preparing herself for what lay ahead, said little.

About thirty minutes later Hart brought his car to a halt on the fringes of the campsite where Tucker, Moore and Ross had met their deaths. Wheeler braked the pickup behind him.

The tree-lined clearing appeared deceptively peaceful in the still-cool sunshine. At its center lay the black smudge of an old campfire and, off to one side, Colonel Fogarty's bright blue Studebaker touring car.

But several things belied the tranquility of the setting. A broken lantern and an unfired twelve-gauge shotgun lay close to the dead fire, beside the buckled, claw- and blood-marked left-side door of the Studebaker. And farther back in tree-shade, they saw three long, narrow mounds of earth, each one marked at its head by a modest pile of stones — the final resting-places of Battista Bianchi's three companions.

Wheeler ran his eyes across the scene, licked his lips and finally said: 'How did you find 'em?'

Hart gestured. 'Two of them were close to the fire. One had been . . . ' He trailed off and glanced at Rachel.

'Go on,' she said.

'One had been decapitated,' he said, 'most likely by the edge of that door. The other one's neck had been broken. There were claw-marks all over his throat.'

'And the third?'

'I found him in the bushes over there. He'd been . . . ' Again he hesitated.

'Come on,' said Rachel. 'Let's hear it.'

'He'd been eviscerated.'

Harmonica frowned, but before he could ask the question Corrigan answered it for him. 'He means disemboweled. That right, Hart?'

'That's right.'

Harmonica swallowed loudly.

'All that proves is that wolves or other such predators came in after they died and set about the bodies,' said Wheeler.

'I don't think so. Take a closer look around. You won't find a single animal track here that wasn't made by the thing that killed them. Whatever predators live in these parts, they've *shunned* this spot, Wheeler. And not only the predators. Listen. What do you hear?'

Wheeler shook his head. 'Nothing.'

'That's right. Not even the birds'll come near this spot. Not even so much as a beetle.'

Wheeler's eyes hooded. 'Shame we can't see the bodies, just to make sure it's the way you say it was,' he said.

'You brought shovels, didn't you? Help yourself.'

Ignoring that, Wheeler said: 'What about those tracks you mentioned?'

'They're not hard to see,' Hart said.

He was right. As they slowly came deeper into the campsite they could see tracks everywhere, all made by the same creature . . . and they were, as Hart had said, unnaturally large.

'Bear?' asked Wheeler.

Corrigan knelt and studied one of them. Four small toes fanned out from a roughly triangular central pad, each tipped with a long claw. He shook his shaggy head. 'Bear's got five toes. They're longer and closer together than these.'

'Wolf, then?'

'Similar. But I've never seen wolf tracks as big as these. These are, what, twelve, thirteen inches long, six or seven inches wide?'

'Are they real?' Wheeler said.

'Huh?'

'Could they have been . . . ' He glanced meaningfully in Hart's direction, then finished, ' . . . manufactured.'

Corrigan shrugged. 'It's always possible.'

Wheeler went over to the bloodstained car door, bent and thoughtfully ran his fingertips along the scratches — more accurately *gouges* — in the dented metal. Then he walked around the far side of the car and examined the twisted, snapped-off hinges.

'Christ,' Harmonica said. 'This place gives me the creeps.'

Wheeler fixed him with a hard look. 'Well, before you swallow Hart's cocka-mamie story hook, line and sinker, let's look at this logically. A bear *could* have torn this door off. It *could* have attacked Tucker and the others.'

'Then where are the tracks?' Rachel said.

'Maybe these *are* the tracks. Maybe the wind shifted the sand, distorted them.'

'*All* of them?' she asked skeptically.

'All I'm saying is, it could have happened that way,' he growled. 'A bear stumbled into camp, they panicked, shot at it — '

'The shotgun hasn't been fired,' said Harmonica, picking it up gingerly.

' — maybe they hit it and that got it ever madder than it already was,' Wheeler continued doggedly. 'It killed them and wolves or coyotes came in and set about the bodies.'

' . . . but didn't leave any tracks,' Rachel said.

'Either that, or your boyfriend here tampered with what little evidence there was,' he countered. He took one more look around, but the campsite revealed nothing of its secrets.

'What now, Mr. Wheeler?' asked Corrigan.

'Well, the colonel sent us to find out what became of Tucker and the others, and I reckon we've done it. Corrigan, you and Harmonica get shovels and dig up the bodies. We'll take them back with us. Least we can do.'

'Leave it,' said Rachel.

'What? We can't just leave the poor — '

'We'll collect them on the way back,' she said.

'What are you talking about?' demanded Wheeler. 'We're *on* our way back, right *now*.'

'You are, maybe. But I'm going on, and I'd be obliged if you, Corrigan, and you, Harmonica, would go with me.'

'But — '

'My father sent Perry Tucker and the others up here to find that mine,' she said. 'Unfortunately they met with some kind of 'accident' before they could do that. I don't intend to make the same mistake.'

Wheeler cocked his head at her. 'You plan to go deeper into these hills in search of a mine that more than likely doesn't even exist?'

'Yes, Harvey. You, on the other hand, are free to do as you wish.'

'That's where you're wrong, Rachel. Your father asked me to keep an eye on you, and that's exactly what I'll do. If *you* go on, *I* go on.'

'Corrigan?' she asked. 'Harmonica? I'll see that there's a handsome bonus in it for you.'

Corrigan answered for both of them. 'We won't quit on you, ma'am.'

'You can count me in, as well,' said Hart, finally breaking his long silence.

Rachel looked at him. 'You don't have to, you know.'

'True,' he said. 'But somewhere along the way you're going to run into

85

something that doesn't want you to go any farther. The same something that killed your men right where we're standing now. And when that happens, I want to be around to see it.'

11

Because the colonel had entrusted him with the original map, Wheeler led the way from there on out. About two hours later the pines gave way to rockier ground and a mile further on he had no choice but to bring the pickup to a halt.

Ahead lay a narrow gorge through which ran a thin, shallow stream bordered on one side by a ragged line of brush. A broad, gentle slope choked with tamarisk and loose shale rose steadily to the left of the stream, a sheer wall of pocked amber rock to the right.

Wheeler got out of the truck and waited for the others to join him. 'Still want to go on?' he asked Rachel.

She nodded.

'Then it looks like we'll be travelling on foot from here on,' he said. 'All right — we'll pack as much with us as we can, but essentials only — supplies and tools, got it?'

Anxious to curry favor, Corrigan said: 'Want me to go out and scout the land up ahead?'

'Hey, I'm not sure that's such a good idea,' Harmonica said hurriedly. 'I mean, I think we should all stick together.'

'You worry too much,' Corrigan chided. 'Forewarned is forearmed, right?'

Wheeler nodded. 'It's a good idea.'

'All right,' Rachel said.

'If I run into any trouble, I'll fire a shot.'

He slung a canteen over one broad shoulder and then set off, leaving his companions to collect their gear and supplies. Soon he was picking a careful path alongside the sun-dappled stream.

After a lifetime spent on the drift, working one menial or seasonal job after another just to eke out an existence, this was his chance to finally make some real cash money and set down some roots, and he was determined to grab it with both hands.

He and Harmonica had met during the Great War. Corrigan had been inducted in the May of 1917 and four months later he'd found himself in the 12th Infantry of the 37th Division, fighting for three weeks solid to take a hilltop village called Montfaucon, which the Germans were using as an observation post.

He'd read afterward that the Americans died at a rate of a thousand a day during that campaign, and he remembered being surprised because it had seemed like a whole lot more. But somehow he'd survived it and so had Harmonica, and that had forged a bond between them that existed to this day.

Of course, it helped that Corrigan liked to give orders and Harmonica was happy to take them. That's how they got along. And when the Armistice was finally signed in November and they were no longer obliged to remain in uniform, they mustered out and went on the drift together.

But Corrigan was now in his forties, and Harmonica was roughly the same age. Corrigan knew they couldn't go on living their nomadic life and avoiding responsibility forever. Hell, the winters were already getting harder to endure.

They needed to start thinking about their future right now, before they got much older.

What they needed was a retirement fund, something like shares in a successful mining operation, say. And to get those shares they needed to suck up to the man who could dish them out — Colonel Fogarty. They had to prove their worth to the colonel's daughter and that jumped-up surveyor, Wheeler, and make themselves indispensible.

It shouldn't be difficult, either. Given what had already happened to Perry Tucker and the others, it was entirely likely that they'd run into trouble sooner or later. When that happened he'd be looking to acquit himself nobly in defense of Rachel Fogarty, whether she needed it or not. Then, when word got back to the colonel, he'd be happy to find some way to reward him.

Corrigan moved quietly for such a big man, and his eyes constantly swept the land in every direction for signs of trouble. The high country seemed curiously lifeless. He'd have expected to see dippers and jays at this time of day, or the tracks of skunk, bobcat, elk and even a diamondback or two. But there was nothing, not even a cockroach or a dragonfly, and all at once the sense of confinement he'd felt on and off ever since they'd entered the mountains returned with a vengeance.

Still, Corrigan didn't scare easy. And he certainly didn't buy Hart's wild claims about some kind of Navajo boogeyman. Besides, he had his get-rich-quick fantasies to keep him occupied.

He pushed on until at last the gorge opened out onto flatland, on the far side of which stood a cluster of ochre-colored buttes. Over the years the elements had worn a series of ragged, horizontal grooves into the rock leading up to them, so that they now resembled a clumsy fight of steps.

Corrigan stopped to take a breather, then slipped the canteen off his shoulder and took a drink. He grimaced. The water was lukewarm, and he decided to swap the canteen for the pint bottle of moonshine whiskey he carried in his jacket pocket.

That was warm too, but even warm it tasted a whole lot b —

He suddenly caught a flicker of movement from the corner of his eye, something moving through the gap between one flat-topped butte and another. But when he turned that way, he saw nothing.

He wondered if it had been his imagination, or maybe just a trick of the sun-bright day. That would make it a whole lot easier to dismiss. But somehow he didn't think it was.

Keeping his eyes fixed on the slope he slipped the bottle back into his pocket and pulled out his Colt. Keeping it pointed ahead of him, he approached the slope cautiously.

'Anyone up there?' he called.

A handful of disturbed pebbles bounced down from the higher ground. He froze.

There! He saw it again — a shadow that looked more like a patch of living oil, sliding from rock to rock, there one moment, gone the next.

'Hey, you there! Not so fast!'

Someone was up there, trying to scare the bejesus out of him. And he wasn't going to stand for it.

He started forward again, digging in and thrusting his way up toward the flats beyond the buttes. The rasp of his own labored breathing filled his ears. It was the only sound.

He was about halfway to the top, chin tucked down into his chest with the effort of climbing, when he spotted the shadow again, sliding across the loose sand right in front of him. His head snapped up again. There was nothing to see.

The idea that he was being toyed with enraged him. Cursing under his breath he kept climbing, determined to catch the bastard and teach whoever he was a lesson.

He topped out, breathing hard, and looked around. Still there was no one to be seen, just a mile-long scattering of cabin-sized rocks. He held his breath and listened. There was no sound. Firming his grip on the Colt, he went forward, step by step.

'I know you're up here, whoever you are,' he shouted. 'Might as well show yourself and be done with it.'

There was a sound behind him. He whirled, saw nothing — then caught the tail end of a shadow vanishing around one of the large rocks he'd just passed.

He swore again, was about to set off in pursuit when he heard it.

A low, guttural sound.

A *growl.*

He turned again, was just in time to catch the tail-end of a shadow vanishing like black silk around the edge of the rock directly ahead of him.

With a snarl of his own he went after it at an ungainly run, came around the rock and was just in time to see the shadow drag itself out of sight around the next boulder.

Angry now, *furious,* he went after it.

An inch or three before it disappeared from sight, the tip of the shadow stopped, right where he could see it.

Whatever was casting that shadow was waiting for him to catch up.

He stopped, too. Stopped, listened.

Ah Christ —

He heard it *breathing.* Breathing slowly through lungs big as bellows.

He kept staring at the tip of shadow, waiting for it to move. It didn't. Whatever happened next, then, was up to him. Four paces, maybe five, and he'd be at the edge of the rock and facing whatever the hell it was. He could empty his gun into it and kill it and that would be an end to it. The colonel would reward him and he could forget all about the get-rich-quick scheme that had brought him up here in the first place, because he'd be set for life anyway.

But what if he emptied his gun into it and *didn't* kill it?

What if it killed *him?*

He thought about the three men who had already died.

Decapitated.

Disemboweled.

'Jack!'

Harmonica's yell made him flinch and instinctively turn toward the sound of his voice. At the same moment something huge and hairy came hurtling around the rocks in a blur, and Corrigan screamed.

12

Down in the gorge, Hart reacted immediately. He broke into a sprint even as the scream was followed by the racketing blast of one shot, a second, a third. Wheeler, instinctively tightening his grip on the late Tom Ross's Winchester twelve-gauge shotgun, wasted precious seconds watching him go, then pinned Harmonica with a finger and snapped: 'Stay here and keep an eye on Miss Fogarty!'

But Rachel wasn't about to stay anywhere. Even as Harmonica turned toward her she started after Wheeler at a run. Not wanting to be left alone, Harmonica followed close behind.

As Hart came out of the rocks he spotted Corrigan sprawled at the foot of the slope. The shadows thrown by the buttes covered him like a cloak. Corrigan looked pale and shaken. His eyes were rolling all over the place, and his mouth was working, but the only sounds he could manage were jumbled and indistinct.

Hart quickly knelt beside him and cradled his head. At first Corrigan flinched at his touch. Then his eyes seemed to sharpen in recognition. Wheeler stamped up and barked: 'What happened?'

Corrigan managed: 'I saw it.'

'Saw what?'

The big man sat up on his elbows and forced himself to look back at the gap between the buttes. 'Whatever Hart called it,' he croaked. 'Yeah. I saw its shadow first, went up to get a better look. Then I . . . I heard it . . . growl. Sounded like a dog. Heard it *breathing*, too. I was . . . I was gonna rush it, *shoot* it. Then I heard Harmonica call my name and when I turned — '

'Here,' said Hart, giving him a canteen. 'Drink.'

The others came to join them. 'What's wrong with him?' Harmonica asked anxiously.

Ignoring him, Hart said: 'Go on, Corrigan.'

Corrigan's eyelids quivered as he remembered the oily, unnatural way the shadow had slipped from one rock to the next.

97

'It *charged* me,' he rasped.

And there it still was, seared into his mind; the fleeting, quick-as-a-blink image of something furry moving fast and fluid, like nothing he had ever seen before.

'It was covered in skins and had the face of — '

The blast of the gun in his fist; the way it had bucked like a living thing as it went off, one, two, three. And the . . . the thing . . . moving at incredible speed, racing past him, vanishing —

'The damn thing moved fast as summer lightning,' he said, 'and it . . . it had a face like the bones of the dead.'

Another vision struck him then — of the thing scaling the almost sheer rock-face of the nearest butte as if it was nothing, still moving in that slipping, sliding wholly unnatural way.

'Corrigan?' Harmonica said softly.

Corrigan looked up, blinking in confusion as he came back from the memory. 'Then it climbed that butte,' he said, 'like it was some kind of spider. But it weren't no spider.'

Breathing heavily now, his face glassy

with sweat, he bowed his head.

Hart said: 'What happened to your neck?'

'Huh?'

As Corrigan looked up again, he became aware for the first time that blood was flowing hot down his neck and staining his shirt-collar. He went to answer but then another flash of memory struck him, and it was a moment longer before he could find his voice again.

'It had claws,' he whispered. 'It slashed at me as it went past.'

'All right,' said Hart, sliding his satchel off his shoulder. 'Sit tight. I'll patch you up.'

'And then what?' asked Harmonica.

'What do you mean, then what?' demanded Rachel, who was standing back, content until that moment just to listen.

Harmonica gestured to Corrigan. 'I've knowed him years, Miss Fogarty. *Years*. I didn't think the thing had been born that could throw a scare into Dan Corrigan. Now look at him.'

'I'll tell you what happened,' said Wheeler, breaking his own long silence. 'He let his imagination get the better of him.'

'That's a hell of a — '

'It's easy enough to do, out here,' Wheeler interrupted. 'And I'm not altogether blaming him. But here he is, way out ahead, all by himself, probably still thinking about all the crazy tales Hart's been spouting. He stops, he thinks he sees something up there, it throws a scare into him — '

' — and then he imagines he's seen a *monster?*' finished Harmonica. 'No way, Mr. Wheeler, sir. Dan's made of tougher stuff than that.'

'He saw *something,*' granted Wheeler. 'That's obvious. But I wonder how much of it was real and how much of it was just imagination.' He halted suddenly, then added with a sudden flare of temper: 'I'll be damned! Smell him! He's been boozing!'

At last some of Corrigan's old spirit returned and he reared up indignantly. 'One drink!' he yelled. 'Now, if you're calling me a liar, Wheeler, you just come right out and say it and we'll settle this here and now!'

Rachel said: 'Quit it, the both of you!'

'Well, I say we go back,' said Harmonica.

'We can't go back,' she said. 'We stand to lose too much.'

'She's right,' Wheeler agreed. 'Besides, if it exists, whatever it is, we can *kill* it.'

'Look at that butte!' cried Harmonica. '*Look!* That's about a hundred and fifty feet to the top, and every inch of the way as smooth as glass. If Corrigan says it climbed that thing, I believe him.'

'But it didn't *kill* Corrigan, and he isn't dead from fright, either.'

'No,' said Rachel, remembering her conversation with Hart in the Palace Café. 'No — it didn't kill him. It was just giving us another warning.'

'One you're fixing to ignore?' Harmonica said.

Hart finished patching Corrigan's wound, then stood up, gathered his gear and headed for the slope.

Watching him, Rachel said: 'Jase! Where do you think you're going?'

A smile touched briefly at Hart's mouth. 'Chasing shadows,' he said grimly.

13

Hart cut crosswise up the slope, but whatever Corrigan had seen there was no longer in evidence. It had left tracks, though — the same elongated wolf-like tracks it had left at the spot where it had killed the colonel's three men, and Hart was kneeling beside one of them when the others finally gathered up their gear and joined him.

'Still think I made it up?' Corrigan asked Wheeler.

'I didn't say you made it up.'

'Imagined it, made it up, it all comes to the same thing,' spat Corrigan. 'Well, there's your proof.'

'Proof that you saw *something*,' granted Wheeler. 'Not that you saw some kind of . . . critter.'

Harmonica's face was suddenly all eyes. 'Take a look at them tracks, Mr. Wheeler, sir! Do *you* know any critter leaves tracks like that?'

Hart straightened up and squinted at the top of the butte. 'It went that way, all right,' he confirmed. 'Just like Corrigan said. You can even see the spot where the tracks end, right at the base of that rock.'

'Well, that suits me just fine,' said Wheeler, consulting his map. 'Because according to this, we've got to go in the opposite direction. And before you get any ideas about going after that creature, 'Jase', forget it. It's like Rachel says — I'll feel happier having you where I can see you.'

Hart only shrugged. 'You still don't get it, do you, Wheeler? I don't have to go after *it*, because if we don't turn around right now, it'll come after *us*.'

★   ★   ★

The long, hot afternoon passed slowly. They trekked across a vast, sandy desert sprinkled with tamarisk and coyote willow, always heading for a range of misty blue mountains that never seemed to get any closer.

Although she was quickly coming to

learn that the high country had a peculiar way of wearing a body down, Rachel stubbornly kept putting one foot in front of the other. The supplies she'd elected to carry seemed to have doubled in weight since she'd first picked them up that morning, but she refused to complain or give in. This was too important. They had to know for sure if the mine was actually there, and if it was, whether or not it was worth the expense of trying to exploit it. But more important still was her need to continue proving her worth to her father.

Oh, she'd proven herself to him time and again, of course, and no son could have done more. But it had taken her years to finally win the colonel's approval, and it was so precious to her that she had no desire to lose it now.

She realized that Wheeler had dropped back to walk beside her, and her mouth tightened with distaste. There had been a time, shortly after Harvey had first come to work for her father, when she had considered him a friend, and eventually much more. He was loyal to the colonel, was good at what he did and always got things done, usually on time and under-budget.

At first he had shown her nothing but courtesy. He'd taken her to the theater in Albuquerque, where her father had his ranch headquarters, and they'd also gone dancing. He'd done everything he could to sweep her off her feet, and he'd succeeded. But it had quickly become obvious to her that she was little more than a stepping-stone to him, simply a means to an end.

For the truth was that Harvey had realized early on that, though he knew he could do well in the colonel's employ, he could do better still as the colonel's son-in-law. As part of the Fogarty clan his future would be assured.

Hurt by the realization, she'd tried to convince herself that she was mistaken, that Harvey's intentions were honorable and that it was her he was really interested in. It was only when she finally did the one thing she'd never done before, and looked him right in the eye, that she saw the truth. He would never truly love her. He might covet her, he might consider her his property, but love . . . ? Love was something Harvey had never experienced and would never truly understand.

They'd argued then, and he'd turned violent and come frighteningly close to striking her. Even now she didn't know how he'd stopped himself. But after that whatever feelings she'd believed she had for him were replaced by something very close to loathing, and she avoided him whenever possible.

Now Wheeler said: 'I hope your father knows what he's let himself in for. If that mine really is up there somewhere, it had better be as rich as he thinks it is, because it's going to cost him a fortune to make it pay. We'll have to cut a road in here, for a start, and that won't come cheap.'

'Few things in life do, Harve,' she replied. 'It's like my father always says. The price of easy is two cents on the dollar.'

Eventually the foothills began to embrace them. Again Corrigan was struck by just how quiet and lifeless they were. It was as if every living thing had decided to clear out until whatever the Indians had summoned up, whatever it was he'd seen and which had slashed his neck as it passed him in a blur, had gone back to wherever it had come from.

It occurred to him that they had the right idea.

The ground continued to rise steadily, but it was only when Harmonica happened to glance back once to make sure they weren't being followed that he realized just how high they'd climbed and how steep the slope had become. For a moment then he knew a giddying sense of vertigo.

Up ahead, Hart came to a halt and the others, breathing hard with exertion, gathered behind him.

'What's up?' Wheeler inquired. 'Why have we stopped?'

'Don't you feel it?' Hart said. He turned and looked at Rachel.

She thought about it, and was about to shake her head when her attention was taken by an abutment of rock at the very top of the ridge. Perched above it, a sinister black growth against the cloudless blue sky, were the remains of a dead tree, an ancient birch that had once been struck by lightning, she thought. Its tall, twisted trunk was supported by a network of gnarled roots that had wound around the stone.

She heard a weird, flute-like sound, or thought she did. It was the same sound she'd heard that night in town, when she'd looked out into the dusty main street and seen the old Indian heading for the Palace Café, a flute that wasn't a flute, a sound that might just as well have come from wind blowing through old bones.

'The tree . . . ' she muttered with an odd sense of wonder.

Hart nodded. 'It's singing to us.'

Wheeler snorted.

'Don't you hear it?' Rachel asked.

'I hear the *wind*,' he said. 'For God's sake, Rae, can't you see he's manipulating you? Making you see and hear what he wants you to see and hear?'

'It's another warning,' Hart said softly. 'Lightning-trees have a special significance to the Navajo.'

No sooner had the words had his mouth than there came a shockingly loud *whump* and the tree burst into flames. Rachel gave a startled squeal as a wave of heat swept down the slope to batter them, and instinctively they all dropped to their knees and covered their faces against it.

A scream tore through the roaring flames, and everyone looked around as Harmonica lost his balance and fell backward, rolling down the slope with increasing momentum.

He made a desperate grab for some low brush, hoping to slow himself, but it tore away in his hand and he started tumbling even faster, his descent now more a series of ill-coordinated somersaults than anything else.

Corrigan bawled Harmonica's name, but it seemed that was all anyone could do. Then Hart flung off his pack and went after him in a series of reckless sideways leaps, each landing sending a wave of loose sand sliding down ahead of him.

Harmonica was falling faster than ever, tipping end over end in a billowing cloud of dust. He looked more like a rag doll than a man.

As the others watched, Hart closed

on him, then dived forward and grabbed at one flailing arm. His fingers closed around the wrist and for a moment Harmonica's momentum dragged Hart down with him. Teeth clenched, Hart struggled to turn himself around, then dug his heels in and they finally slowed to a stop.

Both men lay there, each sprawled flat and gasping for air.

After a moment Hart sat up and looked down at Harmonica. 'You okay?'

Harmonica's face was twisted. Dust clung to his sweat. 'Think I've busted my arm,' he whined.

Still breathing hard, Hart got up onto his knees and carefully inspected the other man's left arm. He didn't think it was broken, but there was no doubt that Harmonica had sprained it and badly bruised the bone. 'You'll live,' he said after a while.

Harmonica looked up at him, his eyes watery. 'Mind if I have that in writing?'

'You all right!' Rachel shouted.

Hart looked toward the ridge and waved.

Beyond the others, the flames were still roaring skyward. Cinders and ash charred the sky and then began to rain down on them like clack snow.

Wondering what had caused the tree to combust the way it had, Hart decided to examine it once it cooled down.

Around them the day was finally waning. They had to find somewhere safe to camp before night fell. He got up and then extended a hand to Harmonica. 'Come on,' he said.

14

Night.

It fell with the dramatic suddenness of high country nights everywhere, and with it the temperature plunged, so they were pleased to hunker around the small fire and drink hot coffee — all, that was, except Hart. He sat off a short distance and by lamplight wrote in his journal.

Wheeler had kept silent for much of the evening. Now he looked up from the flames as Rachel said: 'I need to look that geologist's map over.'

He pulled the map from his leather carry-all and thrust it at her. She unfolded it and started to study it by the meager light.

'Think what you want of Hart,' Wheeler growled, 'but I tell you — '

She looked up at him. 'Let's you and I talk as little as possible, all right?'

He reached out and grabbed one of her hands. She tried to wrench it free but he was too strong. 'In the end you'll see I'm right,' he said.

'Let me go, Harvey.'

He didn't — at least, not immediately. He held on just long enough to make his point.

* * *

On the other side of the camp fear dried Harmonica's lips. He gave up trying to play his mouth organ and stared morosely into the darkness. 'I don't know why we're going on after today,' he said miserably. 'I'd rather be alive than rich.'

'We'll be both,' said Corrigan. He sounded confident, but there was an edgy look in his eyes that Harmonica had never seen before and which refused to go away.

'What do you mean?'

'I was lying earlier,' Corrigan whispered.

Harmonica squinted at him. 'Say again?'

'*Lying*, you fool. I didn't see anything in those rocks this morning. I fired a few shots and screamed out to — '

'What about your neck?' asked Harmonica.

For just an instant Corrigan faltered.

Then he said: 'I did it myself, used my knife, so I'd look the part. Faked those tracks, too.'

'Why'd you do a fool thing like that?'

''Cause we're gonna frighten the others out of these hills ourselves, pal. That, or kill 'em.'

Harmonica eyed him nervously. 'You don't mean that!'

'Kill him, flay 'em, and bring their corpses back with a story that would keep the devil himself out of these hills for a hundred years,' Corrigan said with relish.

In the half-light his face had taken on a satanic hue. That was something else about him that Harmonica had never seen before. Oh, he could be a surly sonofabitch at times, sure he could, but he'd always played fair with Harmonica, and Harmonica knew he wasn't always easy to put up with.

'I still don't get it,' he whispered at last.

Neither did Corrigan, entirely. All he understood was that his encounter with whatever he'd seen earlier today had sharpened his thinking and made him realize that, right now, the risks vastly outweighed the potential rewards. If he was going to continue putting his life on the line, he wanted to make sure it was worth it. Right now there were no guarantees.

Glancing around to make sure there was no danger of being overheard, he said: 'At first I figured we'd set ourselves up for some kind of reward from the old man, the colonel. You know, for sticking by his daughter when things got hairy. But then I got to thinking. That colonel's a mean old cuss, everyone knows it. Who's to say we won't get anything more'n a 'much obliged and fare-thee-well' out of him? Besides, what's better than having a share in something?'

'Having all of it?' Harmonica hazarded.

Corrigan's teeth showed in a tight smile. 'You got it, pard. So here's how we're gonna play it. If these fools don't run screaming from these hills of their own accord, then we've got to trump up something to make 'em. Then we get that mine all for ourselves.'

'*If* it exists.'

'Oh, it exists, all right. Must do. Someone killed Perry Tucker and the others. But not something out of a digger's nightmare.'

It was vital that Harmonica believe that. Corrigan knew if he told him the truth, he'd lose Harmonica for good, and he also knew it would take the pair of them working together to pull this off, especially if it really *did* come to murder.

As Harmonica absorbed what he'd just been told, he realized that Corrigan was smiling at him. Harmonica was part-awed by his friend's plan, and part-scared. Corrigan seemed to take pleasure in both reactions. His neck wound shone red.

Then Corrigan lay back and closed his eyes. Harmonica kept watching him.

'Play something sweet, pard,' Corrigan said, settling himself more comfortably. 'Something I can dream to.'

⋆   ⋆   ⋆

As Harmonica wet his lips and started to play a mellow ballad, Rachel poured coffee into a tin cup and took it across to Hart. He looked up, took the mug and nodded thanks.

'Do you write it all down?' she asked, gesturing to the journal.

'All of it.'

She sat down beside him. 'I hope you won't write too badly of me.'

'Who said I'd write about you at all?'

The reply tipped her vanity a little. 'So,' she said, her tone a little cooler than before. 'What have you found so far?'

'Nothing. I have no answer for why that tree burst into flame. There were no tracks nearby, no lingering smells or other traces of chemicals, no spent matches.'

'How about a magnifying glass? When I was a kid we used to channel the sunlight through a lens and watch the grass begin to smoke.'

'That's considered taboo among the Navajo,' he said seriously. 'They believe that if you start a fire that way, you'll suffer burning in your stomach.'

'Did you just make that up?'

'No, ma'am — uh, Rae. The Navajo are a spiritual people, and they take their beliefs very seriously. They have any number of taboos.'

'Such as . . . ?'

He considered, then said: 'Don't point at a rainbow with your finger, otherwise the rainbow will cut it off. Don't whistle or you'll call up the wind. If a man mimics an animal, he'll become that animal.'

'And you believe all that?'

'No more than I believe that carrying an acorn brings you good luck, or that your boyfriend will leave you if you knit him a pair of socks. But I don't tempt fate any more than I have to.' He looked her directly in the face. 'There *is* something up here, Rae. That's beyond doubt, and you know it. I believe I know what it is. But why does it want to keep us out of these mountains? That's the question.'

She drew a breath. 'Shall I tell you what I think? I think you and Battista Bianchi have one thing in common. Whether it's true or not, you both believe it absolutely. Take that tree, for example.'

'What about it?'

'Well, you said it wouldn't have been started by a Navajo with a magnifying glass because the Navajo consider that taboo.'

'And . . . ?'

'Suppose that tree was set alight by someone who's *not* a Navajo? Suppose the Navajo aren't behind this at all?'

He fell quiet. She might just have a point there. Maybe the light of reason was up to its old tricks again, casting more shadows than it dispelled.

★ ★ ★

Morning.

The sun, just like the five-strong party beneath it, climbed steadily higher. After the chill of the previous night, the new day was hot and uncomfortable. But Rachel seemed more determined than ever to see her self-imposed mission through.

About an hour into the march a sound drifted down from the rocks to the northeast that made them stop and listen. To Harmonica, favoring his left arm, it sounded uncomfortably like old bones clacking against each other.

All at once the discordant sound seemed to grow louder. Hart, frowning, his eyes everywhere at once, sensed the uneasiness of those around him. He felt more than a little uneasy himself, but then went ahead, over the lip of a ridge to the edge of a small bowl of land on the far side that was filled almost to overflowing with bleached and broken bones.

Human bones.

'Jesus,' whispered Wheeler, coming to a halt beside him.

They were stacked three or four feet high in places, and here and there someone had planted tall stakes to which they had fashioned bone wind chimes and mobiles. The bones clacked together and made bizarre music, but there was no breeze this morning, nothing to make them knock and tap against each other. And yet they did.

Rachel came over the rim next, then Corrigan and finally Harmonica. They stood shoulder to shoulder, studying the bizarre tableau in silence. At last Wheeler found his voice again and said: 'Burial ground?'

Corrigan shook his head. 'Can't be. For one thing, whoever these people were, they weren't buried. For another, I doubt there's this many digger Indians in the whole of New Mexico. They must have some of ours and the Spanish here, too. Some of them ribcages look pretty big for a digger.'

Rachel swallowed hard, and to Wheeler's chagrin she turned to Hart. 'Jase?' she asked.

Hart replied quietly: 'This doesn't fit the Navajo at all. For a start, they *always* bury their dead. They wash them and dress them and observe all kinds of rituals because, if the burial's not conducted properly, they believe the corpse's spirit will come back, and that's something they don't care to risk. Besides, once the body's buried, the entire area is wiped clean of prints and the tools used to dig the hole are destroyed.'

'So who does that make these poor souls?'

'Outsiders?' asked Harmonica. 'People like us? People the Indians didn't want up here?'

'If so, they've been keeping their secrets an awful long time,' said Hart. 'Corrigan's right. These bones are unbelievably old. They've been here for decades.'

'How can you tell?' asked Wheeler, hoping to catch him out.

Hart said: 'Take a closer look. There are practically no small bones left, and they're the ones that dislocate and become buried or lost first. All that's left here are the larger bones, femurs, tibias, pelvises and the like.'

'And they're here because . . . ?'

'Another warning?' Rachel asked.

Hart nodded. 'I think so.'

'Well, said Harmonica, casting a scared eye at Corrigan, 'I don't know about the rest of you, but I've seen enough. I think we ought to turn around and go back.'

'Well, you'll have to go back alone,' Wheeler said. 'Me, I'm seeing this through to the finish.'

Harmonica looked like he was about to cry. He looked back the way they'd come. The country was immense, bad enough when you were in company, but worse still if you were all by yourself. He reckoned he could get through the days okay, but after nightfall it might be a different story.

'All right,' he said in defeat. 'You win.'

Hart indicated the thin trail that bordered the dip. 'We'll show these folks a little respect and skirt around them.'

He set off and the others fell in behind him. The bones clacked a little louder, or at least that's the way it seemed. Harmonica, fetching up the rear, twitched a little, certain he was being watched. He took another fearful glance at the bones, saw nothing and was just about to face front again when he noticed —

There was a skull partially buried among the bones, facing his way. For just an instant he thought he'd caught a flicker of . . . something . . . in its shadowy eye-pits. He stopped, looked again, hoping that he was mistaken.

The skull looked back at him, seemingly dead and empty. And yet Harmonica had the oddest conviction that it was no such thing.

And sure enough, in the very next moment —

The skull began to rise up out of the

sea of bones, the body beneath it covered with skins, and it wore some kind of sleeveless hauberk, or tunic, fashioned out of human finger-bones.

Harmonica's mouth opened wide and he screamed.

15

As his scream tore through the air, Hart and the others whirled around. Wheeler and Corrigan both instinctively brought up their weapons, only to freeze when they too saw the apparition rising in the center of the bone-yard, brittle calf bones and ulnas, ribs and sternums tumbling away from it in a calcium landslide to land hollowly around its legs.

It raised its hands and held them out to Hart and the others, and as it did so its mouth opened and it made a howling cry.

At the same time, the stakes holding the wind chimes and mobiles started to tilt and move, and all around them the bones started to heave as if they were reforming. Another figure lifted out of the jumble, and another, and one more.

Wheeler aimed his shotgun at the nearest one but Hart quickly slapped it down. 'They're human,' he said.

Wheeler looked again, saw that he was

right. They were Indians — Navajos — and they were of both sexes and a variety of ages. They were dressed like a host of ghouls from a fever-fed dream, in the gaudy uniforms of slain dragoons and fine silks torn into rags and helmets from the age of the Conquistadors and old blue cavalry tunics frogged and braided and stained with blood. Their faces were painted crimson and white and their hair was plastered with lard.

Wheeler and Corrigan exchanged a look. Wheeler said: 'I say we get them before they get us.'

'You don't think you're going to fight your way out of this?' said Hart.

'We can give it a damn good try,' Corrigan snarled.

The Indians brought lengths of hollowed-out bone to their mouths and began to play some kind of death-song. The sound was like flutes mixed with screams, and Hart had the impression that they were summoning someone, or maybe some*thing.*

At the same moment he felt eyes boring into his back and turned. He was right. There on the slope not fifty feet behind them stood an ancient Indian — the same old Indian who'd caused such an upset back at the Palace Café a few nights earlier.

Silence fell across the scene. Rachel had no idea just how much the sound had grated on her nerves until it finished. Even the bone chimes and mobiles had stopped clacking.

Corrigan turned, saw and recognized the Indian. 'You should've let me put a window in that digger's belly when I had the chance,' he rasped, his thick fingers flexing around the barrel of his Colt.

'Shut up,' Rachel said, 'and hold your nerve.'

'But these're the sonsofbitches who killed your men!'

'We don't know that for sure.'

The old Navajo was holding a jug and a tin cup. He raised the jug and shook it. The sloshing sound it made silenced them.

'Mescal,' he called. Then he pointed to his old military frock coat. It was torn and faded, but the chest was decorated with a staggering array of tarnished medals. He pointed to them and said: 'One medal for every promise broken. One medal for every lie told. One medal for every war we have been made to fight.'

Then he started down to them, his legs sturdy but warped, his free hand resting on the tip of the strange, yard-long twist of blackened wood tucked beneath his belt, and Hart felt his companions stiffen warily. When he was close enough the old man drew up, uncorked his jug, poured a cup of mescal and offered it to Corrigan.

'Drink to your death,' he invited.

Corrigan showed his teeth in a grimace. 'You'd like that, wouldn't you?' he hissed. He held the old man's stare for another long moment, then added: 'You can keep your mescal. *Choke* on it.'

The old man only shrugged and looked at Harmonica. 'You?'

Nervously, Corrigan's scrawny partner shook his head.

'You?' the old man asked Wheeler.

Wheeler said: 'We're not drinking with you, whoever you are.'

He offered it to Rachel. She too shook her head. And finally he came to Hart.

Hart took the cup, peered into it, then

looked at the Indian. 'You have a name, Old One?'

'I am Bidziil.'

'Well, Bidziil, it's not that we're being inhospitable, but we don't intend to put death into our heads and let it wait there.'

Deliberately he poured the mescal onto the ground, where it puddled briefly between the Indian's feet before vanishing into the sand. The old man eyed him curiously.

'You've done something foolish, Bidziil,' Hart went on. 'You've unleashed something that was best kept in darkness, something brutal that's already killed three men that we know of.'

'You know nothing, white man.'

Hart stared him straight in the eye. 'I know about Maii'.'

For an instant the old man's eyes widened almost imperceptibly and it seemed that he rocked back a little on his heels. Then he regained control of himself and said: 'Who are you? How come you to know of Maii'?'

'I seek the truth, Old One. I hear things, I follow whispers. I learn the truth of things for myself.'

'And you have heard of Maii'?'

'I heard that a man named Saxon came into these mountains not so many months ago.'

Beside him Rachel flinched, recognizing the name of the man from whom her father had bought the map.

'I heard that something strange happened to him here that broke his nerve. I came to find out what that thing was, and when I arrived in Jemez Springs I found that it had happened again, this time to a man named Bianchi.'

'And you believe Maii' is responsible for these strange things?'

'I believe you summoned Maii' for reasons I don't yet understand,' Hart replied evenly. 'I believe he killed three men and drove the fourth one out of his mind. And I believe he did this because it was your will. What I don't understand yet is why you want to keep the white man out of these hills.'

Around them, the others waited to see how Bidziil would react to the accusations. He said only: 'You show wisdom,

130

for a white man. But wise men die just as easily as stupid ones.'

Wheeler bulked himself up. 'Are you threatening us, Indian?'

'I am telling you this,' said Bidziil, turning to face him without fear. 'All men have their destiny. Mine is to protect these mountains and do whatever I can to stop that which is unstoppable from coming to pass. I will fulfill my destiny, by any means I can. If you wish to take that as a threat, do so. But know this. I will not rest until the white man shuns these hills, and even then I or someone like me will keep watch to make sure they remain shunned.'

'It might help,' Hart said, 'if you were to tell us why.'

'Even one as wise as you would not understand,' said Bidziil. 'But the decision is yours. Turn and go back where you came from, and you will live. Stay on the path you have chosen and you will die, all of you — and soon.'

He didn't so much look at them then as *into* them. Then he finally turned and marched away, his head held high, his aged shoulders now proudly squared. Behind them, the other Navajos climbed from the bone-yard and melted off into the nearby trees.

'Well, he made *that* plain enough,' Harmonica said. 'Let's go back down now, while we still can.'

Catching his eye, Corrigan nodded. 'Yeah. You heard the man. I'm starting to think Harmonica was right all along.'

'Tie your tongue,' said Wheeler. 'They're just digger Indians done up like a carnival show — '

' — who've just threatened to kill us, Mr. Wheeler, sir!'

'That mine is just as much ours as theirs,' muttered Wheeler.

Rachel had been silent throughout the exchange. Now Hart realized she was looking at him. 'Ma'am?' he said.

'Would *you* keep going if we went back?' she asked.

He looked up the mountain. 'Yes.'

That seemed to decide her. 'Well,' she said with new determination, 'halfway down is just as far as halfway up. We're going on — and Maii' be damned.'

16

That night Harmonica found it impossible to sleep. Every time he felt himself drifting off some sound — the snap of a twig in the fire, maybe the passage of a hunting salamander, assuming such creatures had finally decided to return to the high country — brought him back.

He turned over, and staring up at the stars told himself he should have headed back to Jemez Springs, and to hell with what the others had to say about it. But again he thought about just how bad he'd feel now, after dark, and him all by himself. At least here there was safety in numbers, and he knew Corrigan wouldn't let anything happen to him. Corrigan had looked out for him for years now, and that was just how he, Harmonica, liked it.

But almost before he realized it he found himself wondering just how far he could trust his partner. Corrigan had never let him down before. Then again, he'd never considered murder before, either, and sure as hell that's what he was considering now. *We're gonna frighten the others out of these hills ourselves,* he'd said. *That, or kill 'em. Kill 'em, flay 'em, and bring their corpses back with a story that would keep the devil himself out of these hills for a hundred years.*

He'd meant it, too.

It was a cool, callous side of Corrigan Harmonica had never even suspected before. And if Corrigan was seriously able to consider committing murder to get what he wanted, how long would it take him to realize that without Harmonica around he could have that mine all to himself?

He listened to the night, hoping for sleep but not holding out much hope for it. Around him, the darkness was silent. And yet . . .

He sat up on one elbow, frowning, and listened harder. In the distance, so faint that it could just as easily be imagination, he thought he could hear someone playing a flute. He was sure of it.

He looked around the camp. His

companions were all sleeping. For a moment he considered waking them up. Corrigan might think he was trying to throw a scare into the others and play along with it. But he knew what he could expect from Wheeler. *It's just your imagination, you dummy. Go back to sleep.*

Instead he threw off his blanket, got up and headed into a stand of close-packed alder and birch at the edge of camp, where he judged the music to be coming from.

He walked deeper into the darkness and right past her and yet he didn't see her until she said softly: 'You are a fool.'

He whirled around, startled. She was sitting on a rock, cross-legged, the flute she'd been playing — to Harmonica it looked suspiciously like a human leg-bone — now silent in her lap. She was a lovely young Navajo girl wearing some kind of dress made from beads and bits of glass and mirrors, and when she moved the faint reflections of moon- and star-light flickered and winked off their rounded edges, making her shimmer like a spirit.

'You should have gone back,' she said

when he made no reply.

Although she spoke in her own language, he was somehow able to understand her perfectly. Since he didn't speak Navaho, he knew he should have been surprised. But for reasons he couldn't pinpoint, he wasn't.

Gawking, he glanced to the left and right, but saw that she was alone. She confirmed it with her next statement: 'I need no one with me to talk to a fool.'

'Not so much of your lip, girl,' Harmonica managed at last. 'What . . . what do you want with us?'

'You are a fool who listens to a larger fool,' she said.

Frowning, he took one curious step closer.

'What're you doin' here?'

'I come to warn you.'

He summoned enough courage to snort at that. 'I thought you people warned us pretty good this afternoon.'

'I come to warn *you*,' she repeated. Then, as if she'd read his earlier thoughts: 'Do you think your friend isn't going to kill you, too?'

Harmonica opened his mouth to say one thing, then changed his mind and said something else instead. 'I don't know what you're talking about.'

'Then why are you so frightened?'

'I ain't frightened. Leastways, not of Corrigan.'

'He is going to kill the others and keep the mine.'

'Who told you that?'

'Maii' has walked inside his head.'

Harmonica backed up a step. 'You tryin' to mess with me?'

'No. You will see. Your friend will kill you.'

'That's a lie!'

'There is only one lie,' she said. 'When he told you he did not see Maii' — *that* was a lie. He saw. He just did not want you to run. So he lied.'

Harmonica chewed his lip, troubled.

'It was Maii' who cut his neck,' she continued. 'For now, he needs you to help him kill the others. But in the end he will kill you also, because he knows you are weak, and will fail him.'

The wind blew up and around them

the dry branches clicked together like bones.

'You're the liar,' he said, sounding as if he were trying to convince himself. 'He won't kill me. We're partners.'

Hearing the hollow emptiness of his words, she smiled a smile filled with pity.

'He won't,' Harmonica insisted. 'He might kill the others, but he won't kill me.'

'*Hey!*'

Harmonica spun around and saw Hart walking toward him, holding a lantern high, spilling buttery light all around him.

'Are you all right?'

'Y-Yeah.'

'What are you doing out here alone?'

That jerked Harmonica back to reality. *Alone?*

He turned back to the girl . . . except that the girl was no longer there.

He peered off into the darkness. 'I wasn't alone,' he murmured, frightened. 'I was talking to — '

He turned back to Hart and took the lantern, then stepped farther out into the darkness.

The night was empty. It was as if the girl had never been there.

Harmonica came back, pale-faced. 'Didn't you see her?' he asked hopefully.

'Who?'

'The girl who was sitting on this rock? She was right here.'

Hart eyed him for a long moment. At last he said: 'When I saw you, you were alone, talking to yourself.'

'That's a damn' lie! You must've seen her.'

'I didn't. But that's not to say she wasn't here.'

Harmonica was sweating hard, his eyes worried. He looked up and said: 'Hart . . . what did you hear me saying?'

''He might kill the others, but he won't kill me.''

Harmonica subsided, deflated. He looked badly shaken. 'Do you really believe any of that swill about Maii'?' he asked presently.

'Do *you*?'

Harmonica shrugged and looked away. 'Maybe I was just dreaming.'

Hart watched him walk back to camp.

Then he looked down at the ground. There was only one set of tracks there — Harmonica's. Which left only two possibilities: Either Harmonica had imagined the entire episode . . . or he'd just been talking to a ghost.

17

They were pushing higher toward the peaks next day when Corrigan finally glanced at Harmonica and said: 'What's the matter with you? You've hardly said a word since sun-up.'

Not looking back at him Harmonica said: 'I didn't sleep so good.'

'Well, you'll sleep a whole lot better soon.'

That got a reaction. 'What's that supposed to mean?' Harmonica asked, alarmed.

Corrigan gave him a searching look. 'What do you think it means?' he asked after a moment. 'We'll be rich, pard. And nothing makes a man sleep sounder than being rich.'

Wheeler, meanwhile, had forged out ahead, and was now studying their map and trying to match it up to their surroundings. The country ahead of him was a broken maze of passes.

'Which way?' Rachel asked when she and Hart drew level with him.

'According to this, the original cartographer painted a blue mark on the rocks showing which pass to take.'

'So let's keep a lookout for it,' she said.

Fifty yards farther on Hart spotted it. Then another. And another. And shortly after that it became clear that the Indians had already been there ahead of them and marked twenty or thirty rocks with the same distinctive blue cross.

'Damn!' Wheeler said.

His voice echoed along the maze of canyons.

DAMN . . . Damn . . . damn . . .

Joining them, Corrigan muttered: 'We should have ball and powdered 'em when we had the chance.'

Hart studied his companions for a moment, then leaned against a rock and took a drink from his canteen.

In foul humor, Wheeler said: 'I'll bet you're enjoying this, aren't you?'

Knowing that a reply wasn't really expected, Hart held his silence. But that only infuriated Wheeler even more.

'I bet you'll be putting all this down in your journal tonight, won't you?' he went on, throwing his gear down and coming closer. 'Well, I can promise you one thing, 'Shadow-Chaser' — this wasn't done by your precious shape-shifter! Not unless he carries a can of blue paint around with him.'

Hart finally broke his silence.

'Who are you trying to convince?' he asked. 'Me or yourself?'

Wheeler's volatile temper finally boiled over and impulsively he threw a punch. Hart dodged it easily. Cursing, Wheeler made another lunge, and this time Hart grabbed him by the wrist and executed some sort of blurring flick of motion. In the next moment Wheeler was flat on his back, coughing in the cloud of dust his heavy landing had raised.

Rachel came closer, her face tight. 'Enough! Harvey — give me that map!'

He looked up at her from under lowered brows, eyes bright with anger, and then grudgingly did as she'd asked.

'They could paint every stone from here to creation,' Rachel said, almost to herself. 'But we'll find our way up using spot markings.' Again she looked at Wheeler, who was climbing to his feet and dusting himself off. 'Break out your surveyor's gear, Harvey.'

Wheeler held back for a moment, then grudgingly started toward his pack.

'Hey . . . ' said Corrigan.

Rachel glanced at him. 'What is it?'

Corrigan said: 'Where's Harmonica?'

They looked around, realizing then that the little man was nowhere to be seen.

'*Harmonica?*' yelled Corrigan, and again the echoes mocked them.

HARMONICA . . . Harmonica . . . har-monica . . .

'Get your skinny ass back here right now!'

RIGHT NOW . . . Now . . . now . . .

Around them, the mountains gave nothing away.

'Harmonica!' called Rachel. 'Where are you?'

YOU . . . You . . . you . . .

'Last time I saw him he was bringing up the rear, just like always,' said Wheeler.

They spread out but were careful to

keep each other within sight all the while. Corrigan called Harmonica's name until he was hoarse, but he might just as well have saved his breath.

'The ground couldn't have just swallowed him up,' he said when they regrouped. And yet that was exactly what appeared to have happened.

18

Harmonica's disappearance rattled everyone. For the first thirty minutes they told themselves that he'd simply wandered off and not heard them calling, or just plain gotten himself lost. Any moment now he'd appear over a ridge or the other side of a stand of trees and throw them a wave and when he got close enough to see their expressions, ask them what all the fuss was about.

But as time wore on and there was no sign of him, they realized there was the very real possibility that something bad had happened to whittle their number down to just four.

It was Wheeler who finally broke the moment. 'No sense in wasting any more time,' he said briskly; and breaking out his surveyor's equipment he set about configuring their bearings from the details on the map so they knew which way to proceed.

Rachel picked up one of their skins and took a drink.

Out on the playa, Corrigan continued to yell Harmonica's name and listen to the echoes bouncing back at him. At length even he had to concede defeat and trudged back toward them in a dark mood.

'Neither a track nor a word,' he reported. And then, voicing the thought that was in all their minds: 'It's like something came out of nowhere and carried him away.'

Despite the heat, Rachel shivered. If something *had* happened to Harmonica, it was because she had insisted on seeing this through, and that was a heavy weight to bear. She looked at Hart. 'What do you suppose happened, Jase? Do you think Harmonica came across the same thing Corrigan saw?'

Hart shrugged. 'I don't know. He saw it, I didn't.'

Already on a short fuse, Corrigan immediately bristled. 'I don't like your tone, Hart. It sounds like you're calling me a liar. I know what I — '

Hart said softly: ''He might kill the others, but he won't kill me.''

'Huh?'

'It's something Harmonica said last night. I found him out in the darkness, talking to himself. Except that as far as he was concerned, he was talking to an Indian girl I couldn't see.'

'He was dreaming,' Corrigan said.

'He was awake. *Wide* awake.'

'Well, what do you suppose he meant?' asked Rachel. 'Was he talking about Maii'?'

Hart gave Corrigan a thoughtful look as he replied: 'I really don't know.'

Silence settled like a shroud. Corrigan had an odd expression on his face. 'Well, don't look at me,' he growled. 'I got no idea.'

'Why are you so edgy, then?' asked Hart.

Corrigan's fists bunched. 'Pay attention,' he replied. 'I've just lost my pard and I don't know how.' He threw an impatient look at Wheeler. 'You finished with all your figuring yet?'

'Just about.'

'Well, let's get the hell out of this place. Which way?'

★ ★ ★

With the help of Wheeler's new calculations, they finally found the right pass and took it. It wound like a snake between high rock walls the color of old gold. None of them could shake the feeling of being watched. Every slight rattle of rock, every seemingly restless shadow, every faint, scraping echo held behind it the possibility of threat. Corrigan looked particularly dour.

The sun began its slide toward dusk. And just as they began to think about making camp for the night, they heard a sound drifting toward them from someplace up above.

The lonely, mournful wail of a harmonica.

Corrigan reacted at once. '*It's him!*' he whispered. A relieved giggle spilled from between his whiskery lips. 'Somehow the sonofabitch got *ahead* of us!'

He took off at a stumble-run and

though Hart tried to snag him, he bulled past. By the time Hart took off after him, Corrigan was already vanishing around another bend in the trail.

The pass opened out onto flatland. Corrigan halted and looked around. Ahead and to left and right there was nothing save open ground, bathed now in the powdery cornflower blue of approaching dusk. But he could still hear the faint wail of the harmonica.

Hart came up behind him. Rachel and Wheeler weren't far behind. Corrigan looked around, and even as they listened, the sound finally faded, leaving only silence.

Corrigan yelled: '*Harmonica!*'

This time there wasn't even an echo.

Wheeler eyed their surroundings suspiciously, wanting to doubt the evidence of his own ears but unable to. 'Maybe we *ought* to go back,' he said.

Corrigan turned on him. 'This morning I'd have agreed with you. But now it's different. I'm not leaving Harmonica up here all by himself.'

'Forget it, Harvey,' Rachel said, forcing

herself to remain practical. 'Ten days from now we'll have a hundred miners arriving in Jemez Springs. A hundred miners and equipment, and each man coming on the promise of a job. We don't have a choice.'

'*Harmonica!*' yelled Corrigan.

Nothing.

'Why won't he answer?' Wheeler said, as if thinking aloud.

Rachel looked at Corrigan. 'Are you sure it's him?'

'I've been listening to him play that damn' harmonica for years, ma'am. You think I don't *know?*'

'Then how come he got so far ahead of us? Why is he just playing that one note? And why doesn't he answer when we call?'

'Maybe it's a trap,' said Wheeler. 'Maybe it's someone else playing it, luring us on . . .'

Rachel hardened at the notion. 'Then let 'em try their damnedest,' she said with feeling. 'As far as I'm concerned, we camp here tonight. But tomorrow morning we go on.'

It was fighting talk. But no one slept much that night.

★   ★   ★

Around noon of the next day Wheeler called a halt, again broke out his surveyor's equipment and started to figure out which trail they should take. They had just crossed an upward-sloping yellow grass meadow dotted with the golden flowers of shrubby cinquefoil, and a line of rolling amber mountains now lifted skyward before them.

Hart headed for a winding stream about ten or fifteen yards away and bent to refill his canteen. Once again Wheeler was chagrined to see Rachel follow after him, though he said nothing about it.

As her shadow fell across him, Hart squinted up and said: 'You okay?'

She tucked a stray lock of auburn hair back beneath her hat. 'I'll live,' she said. But it was the wrong thing to say, because it reminded her of Harmonica. 'He's dead, isn't he?' she added softly.

He knew exactly who she was talking

about. 'We don't know that.'

'We do,' she said sadly. 'His disappearance was another warning, wasn't it? Turn back, or else. But I ignored it, and because of that, Harmonica's gone.'

'He might turn up, even yet.'

'You don't believe that any more than I do.'

'All right. Turn back. It's not too late.'

'That's where you're wrong, Jase. And not just because of what I said yesterday, about the men who're coming. If I back down now, turn tail and go back to Jemez Springs, I let everyone down.'

'I don't see that. Your father didn't even expect you to come up here to begin with. Your job was just to find out what had become of your men.'

'That's just it,' she returned. 'Our men. I knew them, Jase. Tucker and Moore, they were as much friends as employees. Tucker, Moore, Ross . . . and now Harmonica. They're all gone because of my father and me, and what's up here. If I turn tail now and admit defeat, it means they died for nothing.'

He wanted to tell her that they'd died or disappeared in order to convince her and her father to forget all about these mountains and the potential fortune they contained. It was her insistence on carrying on that meant they'd died for nothing. But she was pushing herself hard and her nerves were taut. There was no point in making her feel even worse.

'Years ago, in Italy,' he said, 'I read a book by a philosopher named Pietro Pomponazzi. He believed that one man could influence another and in such a way help him achieve things he might otherwise have considered impossible. He argued that life is really a question of *belief*. If you *believe* a thing, you can make it come true. Do you understand what I'm saying?'

She nodded. 'You're saying that Bidziil's working the same trick, only in reverse. Making me believe that what's possible is actually *im*possible.'

'Bidziil or Maii', one of the two.'

Suddenly some talus slid down the rock face behind them. They both looked around but saw nothing. A moment later

Wheeler called: 'Say, where's Corrigan?'

Rachel's first thought was: *Please God, not again.* But as she and Hart turned to the stocky surveyor they realized that Corrigan was indeed nowhere to be seen.

Looking around, Wheeler yelled: '*Corrigan!*'

Hart remembered the sliding talus and turned back to the hills — in time to see Corrigan appear from behind a shelf in the rock about halfway up the steep incline. Cupping his hands to his mouth he called the big man's name. The high country swallowed the sound whole, but not before Corrigan stopped, turned back and beckoned for them to come up.

'You hear it?' he yelled back. 'The harmonica?'

Hart listened. Rachel and Wheeler did likewise. But they, like he, heard nothing. Behind him Wheeler called: 'Get back down here!'

Corrigan pointed upward. 'But he's right over this ridge! Come on! He might be in trouble!'

Without another word he turned and

started climbing again. Hart dropped his gear and said: 'Stay here and keep together.'

Then he started racing toward the foot of the hill.

19

Corrigan had been watching Wheeler make all his calculations without really watching him at all. His mind had been elsewhere, his thoughts on Harmonica, on where he was right now and whether or not the Fogarty girl had been right, and if whatever had stolen him away was the same thing he'd seen among the rocks.

Harmonica could be a pain at times, but they'd been together a long time and Corrigan had gotten used to having him around. Not knowing if he was alive or dead or in need to rescue affected him deeper than he'd thought possible.

At first he'd thought his ears were playing tricks on him again. He wasn't *really* hearing the wail of the harmonica, it was just wishful thinking. He reached for his bottle of moonshine — now closer to empty than full — and rinsed his dry mouth.

But the sound of the harmonica was still there, wailing mournfully like the whistle on a departing train. It sounded so real, all at once he had no doubt that it was indeed a physical sound and not just something in his head.

He opened his mouth to ask Wheeler if he could hear it too, but Wheeler was squinting through the theodolite he'd set up on its tripod and muttering bearings to himself.

Instead Corrigan narrowed his eyes and looked around. Near as he could tell the sound was getting louder, but none of the others were giving any sign that they could hear it, too. He was sure he wasn't going crazy, and was about to call to the girl and that other guy, Hart, when suddenly the sound of the harmonica started mixing with something else, a voice —

Hey, Corrigan.

Harmonica's voice.

Corrigan's eyes bugged and shuttled everywhere, but there was no sign of his partner.

He might kill the others, said the voice,

coming from nowhere and everywhere at the same time, *but he won't kill me.*

Corrigan murmured: 'Harmonica . . . ?'

Was *that* what all this was about? Had Harmonica taken off because he thought Corrigan might not stop at killing Rachel, Wheeler and Hart; that he might decide to kill Harmonica as well? Damn! Didn't that fool know him better than that?

If that was the trouble, he had to set Harmonica straight. *Lord, you do try a man's patience,* he thought, *and there's been plenty times when I could've happily killed you, but I never would've done anything about it. Dammit, man, we're partners!*

Almost before he was aware of it he was heading for the hills, following the mixture of voice and music. As he began to move from a walk to a trot, he scoured the ridge and was finally rewarded by the sight he'd been so anxious to see — Harmonica, playing his mouth organ and hopping from one leg to another in a clumsy jig.

He was running then, all his bone-deep exhaustion leaving him, one only thought uppermost in his mind — to catch up with Harmonica and set him straight and then cuss him good for worrying the life out of him!

Above him, Harmonica danced back out of sight.

Unthinking, Corrigan went after him.

* * *

Get back down here, Wheeler had said. Corrigan paid that no mind. Harmonica was up there, alive but somehow not quite himself. Corrigan figured that something had happened, maybe he'd fallen and cracked his head and it had made him a little crazy. He needed help before he could injure himself any worse.

So he kept climbing, and he went up the grade so easily it felt more like climbing stairs than picking a way across a rock- and brush-strewn incline. He reached forward, closed his big hands around anything that would give him purchase and kept hauling himself toward the ridge. Behind him, dirt and rocks rolled and bounced down toward the golden meadow below.

Without warning he topped out and fell flat on his face. Now that he'd stopped climbing he started gasping for air. He scrambled up and staggered on.

A slope trended down toward a wide bowl of grassland in which sat a small Navajo village. He knew it was Navajo because it was filled with their distinctively round, conical-shaped hogans, each with its doorway facing east to greet the rising sun.

Harmonica was standing in a cleared area at the center of the village. He was no longer dancing, but as soon as he saw Corrigan he started waving him down. It looked as if he'd found something important. Wondering what it could be, Corrigan went down the slope in a trot that made his belly bounce.

He was almost to the edge of the village when it occurred to him that, aside from Harmonica, the place was deserted. The air should have been rich with the smells of cooking, the squeals and laughter of children playing. Men should have been standing in groups, talking, their women sitting in doorways, weaving.

There was none of that.

Indeed, as he jogged deeper into the village, he realized that every doorway was sealed shut.

Corrigan slowed to a more cautious walk. He knew a little about the Navajo. They were, as Hart had said, riddled with superstition, much of it associated with their distinctive dwellings, which were essentially thick mud-walls built up around stout log frameworks.

One such taboo dictated that, should a death occur in a hogan, it becomes the deceased's burial-place and the entry sealed to warn others against disturbing their rest. Even if the corpse is removed (always through a hole in the north-facing wall), the hogan was abandoned and often burned to the ground.

The fact that all these structures were sealed up told him that they had all been used for the dead — that somehow an entire village had died up here and been sealed away before the survivors moved on.

A sound made him start. Harmonica

was whispering to him again.

Over here, pard! Over here!

And playing beneath the whisper was the same doleful moan of Harmonica's mouth organ.

'Where are you, pard?' called Corrigan.

Over here! Look!

Corrigan turned, saw a flash of creased denim — Harmonica's jacket — pass between two hogans and went right after him. Around him the village was a cemetery in all but name, the conical homes of the once-alive now the mausoleums of the long-dead. He weaved between structures, his breath a sawing rasp, finally came out on the edge of the central area and saw Harmonica waiting for him on the far side.

'You sorry sonofagun!' panted Corrigan. 'Where the hell you been all this time?'

Harmonica only waved him on, his movements urgent, and Corrigan ignored the stitch pricking his side and jogged across the sand toward him.

He didn't see the pit until the last minute. It had been covered in branches and leaves, the leaves covered with sand so that it all melted into one.

By the time he stepped into it, it was too late.

The entire structure gave way beneath him. He gave a startled yell and felt himself falling. Earth walls blurred past. Legs kicking, arms flailing, he tried to save himself but there was nothing to grab hold of. The sky, a ragged circle above him, rapidly grew smaller, smaller —

He slammed against the bottom of the pit and screamed as both legs snapped and his left arm dislocated. Dust and dirt sprayed up around him and then slowly settled back over him, coating his eyes, lips and tongue with a fine, gritty film.

The pain was so intense that Corrigan blacked out for a moment. Then a vicious, searing white-hot pain stabbed through him, bringing him back to howling con-sciousness. How long he lay there, sobbing, he had no idea.

After a while his jangled nerves started to settle and he studied his surroundings through glazed eyes. The shaft was about eight feet around, its walls clumpy and rough. He might have used some of those clumps as hand-holds and somehow climbed out, if he'd still had the use of his legs. But his legs were now bent and buckled beneath him, reminiscent of the colonel's.

He stared up at the sky. It looked so bright, so blue, so far away. Wetting his lips he tried to yell Harmonica's name, but all that came out was a croak. He swallowed and licked his lips, tried again.

'H-Harmonica! Pard, you h-hear me?'

There was no response. Only silence. Then he heard a faint trickling sound as dirt drifted down the walls of the pit.

'Harmonica — you gotta help me! I'm in a f-fix, down here!'

I'll help you, pard, said a voice.

Corrigan started. 'Where are you, dammit? You gotta get me out of here! I've busted both legs and my left arm's gone numb!'

I'm right here, said the voice.

And it was.

It was right next to him, so close to his ear that he could feel the breath that accompanied the words.

He whirled around and there was Harmonica, right beside him.

Dead.

He was sitting with his back to the wall of the pit no more than three feet away, hands twisted around his old harmonica, head on backwards, bugs crawling through his hair, a snake slithering slowly across his chest.

Horrified, Corrigan was about to scream when the pit suddenly darkened. He looked up instead, thinking it might be Hart, or Wheeler, come to rescue him.

It was neither.

It was the thing that had killed Harmonica.

Maii'.

With a snarl the shape-shifter dropped down into the pit and landed nimbly astride him with a rattling of bones and a swaying of pelts.

For one terrifying moment it stared down at him. Sunlight flared behind it, throwing it into silhouette. Corrigan's blood ran cold.

Then the creature's lips wrinkled back, baring its long, yellow teeth as it snarled at him. Corrigan smelled its rancid breath, redolent with a thousand nights of feasting on carrion flesh, and he started babbling.

In the next second Maii' was upon him, tearing the clothes from his flesh, the flesh from his bones.

20

Hart spotted the tracks first, with their large, triangular pads, four splayed toes and claws as big as cargo hooks. They led him all the way to the pit. He approached it warily.

It was only as he drew closer that he heard the flies. There was a whole swarm of them down there, if the volume was any indication, and they were the first signs of life he'd encountered since reaching the spot where Tucker, Moore and Ross had met their fate.

When he was close enough he peered cautiously over the rim and frowned. He couldn't see much because the shadows were too deep, but the metallic stench of spilled blood was unmistakable.

His intake of breath was a sharp sound in the otherwise heavy, near-total silence of the village-turned-burial ground. He slipped a coil of rope off his shoulder and looked around for something to attach it to.

The remains of a large loom stood beside one of the hogans. He wasn't surprised. The Navajo, predominantly farmers but later herders of sheep, were also skilled weavers.

The loom still looked pretty solid. Hart tied one end of the rope around the stoutest log and dropped the other end into the pit.

He tied a kerchief around his lower face, tested the rope and then slowly backed over the rim. Holding tight, he rappelled to the bottom of the pit, dreading what he was going to find.

The air was stale and tinny, even through the kerchief. Disturbed flies rose up in an explosion. He tried to ignore them, but it was impossible.

At last he touched bottom and turned around. Corrigan lay on his back with his legs folded unnaturally beneath him. His dull eyes were staring sightlessly at the sky. There was blood around his mouth.

Below the neck his torso had been ripped open and beneath the network of broken ribs a number of his organs were missing. For just a moment Hart felt lightheaded, then fought it off.

Harmonica lay next to Corrigan, his head twisted around on a shattered neck. Hart let his breath go in a soft sigh that puffed at the kerchief across his mouth, then knelt and did his best to examine the corpse.

'Jase?'

He looked up, called: 'Down here!'

A few moments later Rachel and Wheeler appeared above him.

'What happened?' asked the surveyor. Hart was glad to see he had the shotgun in his work-toughened hands.

'Hang on. I'm coming up.'

By the time he'd pulled himself out of the hole the sunlight was almost blinding to his gloom-accustomed eyes. He got to his feet, dusted himself off and tore the kerchief from his face. They watched him expectantly.

'They're both down there,' he said. 'Both dead.'

Rachel paled visibly. 'Harmonica?' she asked. 'How did he get so far ahead of us? And why — ?'

'Did he lure Corrigan to his death?'

finished Hart. 'I don't believe he did, Rae.'

'Are you saying Corrigan imagined it?'

'Maybe. Or maybe what's up here with us put the idea into his head and let his conscience do the rest. But it wasn't Harmonica he was chasing. As near as I could tell, Harmonica's been dead for at least twenty-four hours.'

Wheeler grasped the significance immediately. 'Since he went missing yesterday.'

Hart nodded.

That decided Wheeler once and for all. 'Then I say we go back.'

Rachel didn't answer. She was peering thoughtfully into the shadowy pit.

'Are you listening to me?' he demanded, grabbing her and turning her around. 'Let's leave this madness for someone else.'

She studied him for a long moment, then treated Hart to an equally lengthy examination. Finally she said: 'You two can do whatever you want. I'm going on.'

'You're crazy!'

'Maybe. But there's no one else to leave it to.'

She rummaged in her pack until she

171

found what she was looking for — a small snub-nosed revolver.

Shaking his head, Wheeler said scathingly: 'You don't suppose that'll do much good against whatever left these tracks?'

'I don't know. But it's all I have and I don't know how else to deal with this.' She turned to Hart. 'Do you? 'Cause if you do, tell me.'

'Why ask him?' Wheeler said.

'Because I can trust him.'

'And you can't trust me?'

'I think we settled that question a long time ago, Harve.'

As Wheeler stormed off, Rachel said to Hart: 'If this Maii' thing wants us dead, why the hell doesn't it just kill us and be done with it?'

'For the same reason it spared Bianchi,' he said. 'It wants us to go back and warn everyone else to stay away.'

'But *why?*'

'I don't know,' he replied. 'Maybe — '

'*Maybe,*' Wheeler echoed mockingly. 'Maybe once we went past that sand painting we got lost in hell. Maybe we've gone mad already and don't know it.

Maybe we're already as dead as Corrigan and Harmonica.'

'Shut up, Harvey.'

'Yes, ma'am. Anything you *say*, ma'am. Your time honored servant will go and get himself a *drink*, ma'am.'

Going over to their skins, he glanced back at them. 'Hey, Hart. You know all about these diggers. Is it right that they use herbs and roots to make drinks that can make whoever drinks 'em think he can see demons that aren't real?'

Hart nodded.

'Well, that's real interesting. You know why? Because I've never once seen you take a drink from any of our skins. You've always used your own canteen.'

'You got a problem with that?'

'I do when it looks to me like you don't *want* to drink from our skins.'

'Harvey — ' Rachel began.

But the seed of suspicion had already started to flourish. 'Maybe you spiked our water to help your digger friends. Maybe we've only seen and heard what you've wanted us to see and hear all this time.'

Rachel hurriedly stepped between them.

'You're not making any sense, Harve.'

'No?' He held the skin out to Hart. 'If I'm not making sense, then have this drink on *us*.'

'You've got yourself turned around in more ways than you can count,' Hart told him evenly. 'And you're not doing yourself, or us, any good.'

'Then drink.'

Before he could take the skin, Rachel snatched it out of Wheeler's hand and threw it aside.

He turned on her. 'Why did you do that?'

'Because I don't believe Jase would do what you've said.'

'Oh, no?'

'No.'

'That's ripe. You didn't think he was so honest back in town.'

'No. But I at least know when I'm wrong, and when to admit it.' She looked at Hart. 'We're going on, aren't we?

He went over and picked up the discarded skin, then put it to his mouth and took a generous pull at its lukewarm contents. 'Satisfied?' he asked Wheeler.

And then, to Rachel: '*I'm* going on, sure.'

'Well, that makes two of us. Harvey, you can go with us or you can go to hell. What's it to be?'

He grinned coolly. 'I'll do both, Rae . . . Because up yonder . . . that's where we'll *find* hell.'

★　★　★

They stopped again in the middle of the afternoon and Wheeler consulted the map, then started searching around for landmarks. Although he was still in a foul mood, he went about his work with a cold, unerring eye. Finally he turned to Rachel and Hart, who were resting up in shade a few yards away and announced: 'I'm sure you'll both be happy to know we'll make it by dusk.'

Rachel nodded. 'Thank you, Harvey.'

He doffed his hat sarcastically and began collecting up all his gear.

They pushed on. It was probably just imagination, but it seemed to Rachel as if the land itself were trying to make the last leg of the journey as hard as possible. The sun dipped lower but there was no let-up in the heat. Rachel stubbornly kept going, dead on her feet, but determined to see this through to the end . . . no matter how bitter that end might prove to be.

'*Hey!*'

It was only when she heard Wheeler calling to her as if from a great distance that she realized she'd actually been dozing on her feet. As she jerked back to full awareness she saw that he was standing on the lip of an uneven ridge about thirty yards above them and pointing urgently at something that was presently out of her sight.

She gathered what reserves she still had and took the remainder of the slope at a labored run, allowing Hart to grab one of her arms and help her the last few feet.

It was worth it.

As they topped out they saw the mine ahead of them, a ragged, shadow-choked hole dug out of the copper-colored rock wall before them. Hart stopped to catch his wind but Rachel continued on, past Wheeler, until she finally drew to a halt a yard or so from the entrance.

'A sweet moment, I'm sure,' murmured Wheeler.

She turned but looked right past him to Hart, and that only dug deeper into Wheeler's gut and stoked his already-simmering hatred.

Hart dropped his gear and approached the mine entrance slowly.

'Have I done my job?' Wheeler asked.

Finally, Rachel looked at him. 'What? Oh, yes, Harvey. Yes. Thank you.'

'Then I'll leave you both to it,' he said.

He turned but she moved quickly to stop him. 'Harvey! Don't be a fool. This is as much your triumph as anyone's. Stay with us.'

He yanked his arm out of her grasp. 'Not after what I've seen on the way up here.'

He shouldered his gear and headed back for the ridge. His mind was made up, and all they could do was watch him go.

21

It was already heading toward dusk; too late to do anything but make camp, fix something to eat and then crawl into their blankets.

Night fell quickly and so did the temperature. As they spooned up canned stew, Rachel said to Hart: 'Come morning, look around and satisfy your curiosity about whatever it was that brought you up here. But when you're done, we're going back down and I'm going to tell my father that the mine was all played-out.'

He frowned, surprised.

'I don't want anything to do with this place, not now, not ever,' she continued. 'It's evil. You can almost smell it.'

'If you don't exploit it,' he reminded her, 'someone else will.'

'Well, that's up to them. All I know is that after everything that's happened, I don't want my father or me to have any part of it. And it just might work. Rumors have a way of spreading, Jase, and mining is a competitive business. No one wants to waste time and effort — or money, of course — on a mine that's had its day.' She looked at him across the fire, adding: 'Well? What do you think?'

'I think I was right about you from the start,' he said.

'Meaning?'

'There's hope for you *yet*, Miss Fogarty.'

Her smile died before it could properly be born. They both heard a sound off in the darkness, the hollow rattle of a rock tumbling down a slope. Rachel stared at him, her expression asking the question. Hart peered out into the night, watching, waiting . . .

They didn't have to wait long.

A fist-sized lump of rock rolled down off the ridge above the mine entrance and bounced to a halt at the very edge of the fitful firelight.

Hart reached for one of their lanterns and got to his feet. 'Stay here,' he said quietly. 'I'll go take a look around.'

'Don't go too far,' she warned.

He walked softly into the night, holding the lantern high. It spilled yellow light drunkenly across the sand ahead of him. throwing elongated shadows over the surroundings rocks. Every so often he stopped and listened, but now all that could be heard was the soft sigh of the cool high-country breeze.

He moved on, edging around a bend in the narrow trail that was hemmed in by a larger spill of boulders. Still nothing. Again he stopped, listened. He looked back over one shoulder, realized that he was no longer in sight of camp and decided to head back.

As he turned he heard it leap out of the darkness to his left toward him. He turned back just as it struck him a wide, sweeping blow that knocked him off his feet. He hit the ground, momentarily stunned, the lantern landing with a metallic clank nearby. He recovered quickly but before he could defend himself it was on him, its weight slamming the air from his lungs, and in the lantern light he finally saw his assailant.

It was Wheeler.

The surveyor reared back, Tom Ross's pump-action shotgun now held tight in both fists. He brought the weapon down hard, hoping to crush Hart's skull with the stock. Hart saw moonlight glimmer off the barrel, then twisted sideways to dodge it.

He didn't quite make it.

The weapon caught him a glancing blow on the temple, hard enough to make him see stars but not render him unconscious. With a grunt he unseated his opponent and then groped to his feet.

Wheeler came up at the same time and with a snarl hurled himself back into the fray. Hart ducked the first angry swipe of the shotgun but finally took the stock in the stomach. Wheeler followed it with another blow. Then while Hart was still bent double, he slammed the butt against the nape of his neck.

Pain exploded in Hart's skull and his legs turned rubbery. Wheeler grabbed him by his shirt and propelled him forward. Before Hart could recover Wheeler broke into a run and Hart had no choice but to go with him.

He opened his eyes, saw the sand rushing backward beneath his stumbling feet, and fought to clear his head long enough to stop his headlong flight. But it was already too late for that. The ground vanished beneath Hart's feet and he felt Wheeler throwing him forward, off the edge of a long drop.

He fell, and continued falling for a very long time.

22

Rachel stared out into the night, her small fingers flexing around the grips of her pistol. She wished now that she'd gone with Hart. She'd watched as his lantern grew steadily smaller and finally vanished behind some rocks, and then all she could do was hold her breath, pray that everything would be all right, and watch the darkness for his return.

A minute turned into two, then five, then ten. And still he didn't come back. She nervously licked her lips, went to call his name but the sound died in her throat. If something *had* happened to him, all she would do by calling his name was advertise her own presence here.

But it was impossible to remain silent for long. As much as anything else, the silence began to press on her nerves, and when she finally heard the sound of someone coming toward her out of the darkness she got to her feet and called hopefully: 'Jase?'

'Even better than Jase,' said Wheeler.

At the sound of his voice she aimed her gun toward him. But before she could pull the trigger he came at her from one side, grabbed her wrist and squeezed hard. Rachel winced and cried out, dropped the weapon.

'Well, darlin',' Wheeler said, grinning. 'Shall we pick up where we left off?'

She tried to pull her wrist from his grip, but he was too strong. 'Where's Jase?' she asked defiantly.

Wheeler only grinned at her.

'Let go of me,' she demanded.

Abruptly he brought his free hand up to grab her face. 'No, Rae,' he snarled. 'You've humiliated me once too often. Now it's *my* turn. And you're going to do exactly like I say.'

He tried to drag her down to the ground. She grunted and struggled against him. But he was bigger and stronger than her and eventually she had no option but to fall to her knees before him.

'I may not be perfect, but I'd have treated you right, Rae,' he said, his words thick with emotion. 'All right, so we argued and I lost my temper, but I didn't *hit* you, did I? I said I was sorry and that it wouldn't happen again. You could have given me a second chance.'

While he spoke she felt around behind her, trying to find a rock, a stick, anything she could use as a weapon against him. There was nothing.

'I mean, I've got my pride,' he said.

As she looked up at him and started to make one final attempt to reason with him, she caught a hint of movement in the darkness behind him. For one heart-stopping moment she thought that it was Hart. But then her expression slackened, the blood drained from her face.

She whispered: 'Dear God . . . '

She started shaking so hard that Wheeler hesitated momentarily. He frowned down at her, saw that she wasn't even looking at him, but at something behind him. He wondered if it was Hart, if he had some-how survived his fall.

Then an icy thought hit him.

Maybe it was something even worse . . .

Panicking, he released his grip on

Rachel and spun around.

He thought: *Aww Christ no, no, no . . .*

An instant later Maii' grabbed him, pulled him close and bit his face off.

★   ★   ★

Hart came to with a start. For the first few seconds he had no idea where he was or what had happened to him. Carefully he rolled over, found himself staring up at a starry night sky that looked close enough to touch. He sat up slowly and checked himself for injuries. Aside from a few cuts and bruises and a pounding headache, nothing was broken.

He reached out, steadied himself against a rock and struggled to his feet. His thinking was becoming clearer now. He remembered being attacked and cursed himself for underestimating Wheeler. Then he thought about Rachel, left all alone up there by the mine, and forced himself to ignore the nauseating throb caused by his every movement and set about climbing.

It took him twice as long as it should have. He was still groggy and he had no clear idea where he was. All he knew was that he had to climb, and in the dark that was no prospect to be taken lightly. He climbed, stopped when the world started to tilt and then continued when the nauseating sensation passed. The slope was etched in moonlight. Steam clouded his breath.

At last he reached flat ground and tried to get his bearings. There was no way he would have found his way back to camp if he hadn't seen the fire winking in the distance. Drawing a relieved breath, he headed for it at a jog.

As he drew closer he caught sight of the body hunched against the rocks just beyond the firelight and his throat tightened.

'Rae?'

His voice was a whisper.

He stopped dead when he saw the all-too-familiar tracks in the dirt, quickly checked his surroundings. Only when he was satisfied that whatever had left them had moved on did he cross the camp and kneel beside the body.

He saw now that it was Wheeler,

crumpled against the copper-colored rock wall as if flung there. He put a hand on the surveyor's shoulder and carefully turned him over. When he realized the man no longer had a face he gave a choking cough and fought unsuccessfully to control a sudden bout of nausea.

'Jase . . . '

He recognized Rachel's voice immediately, wiped his mouth and turned in its direction. She was looking at him from the shadows of the mine entrance, barely twenty feet away. Grateful to leave the body, he joined her.

'You all right?' he said. Then as she nodded: 'What happened?'

'I saw it,' she said, badly shaken, her eyes liquid in the darkness. 'Jase, you were right! It *is* Maii'.' She broke off, trying to control her trembling. 'Corrigan was right too . . . it *is* some kind of horrible monster. Draped in skins, with a face like bones — '

'Shhh,' he said, taking hold of her. He felt her shiver in his arms. 'It's all right, Rae. I'm here now.'

'It p-picked Harvey up and . . . and . . . '

'Shhh,' he repeated. He looked around, trying to check their surroundings. But for all he could see he might just as well have been blind.

'I felt sure it w-would kill me t-too,' she said, stammering over every word as the shock of what she'd witnessed finally struck home. 'Oh, dear God, I was . . . b-but there was nowhere to run, so I . . . I hid in here. I know it saw me, b-but it didn't come after me. It fed on Harvey . . . it *fed* on him, Jase! . . . then it turned and walked away, just like a man, but not a man at all. Not even an animal!'

'Easy,' Hart said softly. 'Try to calm down . . . '

She fell silent, emotionally blown-apart, and he sat beside her, held her close and because he could think of nothing else to do, he gently stroked her hair.

'You're safe now,' he whispered, although neither of them really believed that. 'We'll stay put until sunrise, and then pull out, head back to Jemez Springs. All right?'

She shook her head. 'It won't let us, Jase. It intends to kill us all.'

He was about to lie again, to assure her

that they would be safe, when he heard the faint but trilling whistle of a bone flute.

He sat forward, trying to pinpoint its source, and as he did he realized that he wasn't as blind as he'd first thought, because there was a very faint glow coming from deeper in the tunnel.

'Stay here,' he whispered. He tried to pull loose from her but she refused to let go. He firmly gripped her arms, breaking her hold, and whispered: 'I need to find out what's down there.'

'It's Maii',' she said.

'I hope so,' he replied. 'Because that means we can pull out right now, instead of waiting for sunrise.'

She considered that briefly, then decided: 'I'm coming with you.'

There was no time to argue about it. 'Okay. Quiet as you can, though.'

They stood up and crept lightly toward the faint illumination. As they drew closer, he realized that the light was coming up from the ground . . . no, not the ground, but from a down-sloping shaft that was set into the left-side wall. From here he could hear the sound of the flute a little louder.

They entered the sloping tunnel. After some indeterminate distance its roof dropped so low that he had to bend forward to avoid scraping his scalp. He kept one hand touching the wall, the left gripping Rachel's right. The wall and the faint red glow up ahead were his only guides.

Without warning, the flute stopped playing.

They froze, listening intently. It was hot down here, unpleasantly so, and Hart felt rock-dust sticking to his sweat.

Five minutes passed. He considered turning back but didn't. He started moving again with Rachel right beside him.

At last the shaft opened into a cave, at the center of which burned a small, smokeless fire that made fitful shadows stir and caper across the seamed brown walls.

Hart looked around. As near as he could see the cave was unoccupied. Then, from the edge of his vision he thought he saw movement. His head snapped that way, and he told himself that he must have been mistaken.

But he wasn't.

A figure detached itself from the darkness and came forward to confront him.

23

The old Indian, Bidziil, was holding a bone flute between his long, wrinkled fingers. It looked to Hart as if it had been fashioned from a human arm-bone.

After a moment he set it down beside the twisted yard-long length of wood he normally carried tucked behind his belt. Hart frowned, wondering for the first time if the stick was what he thought it was. Then Bidziil spoke, distracting him.

'I knew I would see you again, white man. I saw it in your eyes. A curiosity that would not be denied.'

'It's like I told you before,' Hart said. 'I'm a searcher. I go after the truth.'

'Even if you cannot possibly understand that truth?'

'Why not try me?'

'It is too late for that, white man. It is enough that I have been given an impossible task that I must carry out by any means possible.'

'Including murder?' asked Rachel, finally finding her voice. 'Because that's what you've committed.'

'What are the lives of a few compared to those of millions?' he countered.

It would have been easy to back down. But Rachel dug deep, found reserves she never knew she possessed and faced him square-on.

'In the morning we plan to leave this place, and when we get back to Jemez Springs I'm going to tell my father that he should forget all about his plans for the mine, because it's worthless, played-out.'

'From the white tongue has come many lies,' noted Bidziil.

'Not this time.'

The old man eyed them for a long moment as if they were children. 'Your word is not enough,' he said at last. 'Your father is a stubborn man. It will be hard to convince him to leave this land. And even if you succeed, there will always be others. They will need to learn, as you have. And the voice of death is the only one they will heed.'

'You're wrong,' Hart said.

'How so?'

'Four men came out here at the start. Because of you, because you summoned Maii', three died and the other went back scared out of his wits. But that didn't stop the rest, did it? More came. Five of us, this time.'

'And now only two remain. And soon, not even two.'

'Why?' Hart persisted. 'What's so important about this place that you have to kill whoever comes up here?'

'Because it is my job to change the future,' Bidziil said heavily, 'even though you and I both know the future can rarely be changed.'

'Then why try, Old One?'

'Because it has been foretold that this land will suffer a dreadful fate — that it will bear a terrible, destructive fruit . . . an ungodly force . . . unless I can keep the white man away from it.' He paused, his lidded eyes staring straight ahead as if he could see something they couldn't; then he continued.

'Thus far we have been lucky. Those we have not turned back, Maii' has killed.

But still they come, the whites. I realize now that they will always come.'

'You're right,' Hart said. 'The future can't be changed, Bidziil. The best you can hope for is to make it a better one . . . and you can't do that by killing people.'

'Nevertheless, I have to try. It is my sacred duty.' He looked directly into Hart's eyes. 'The girl's father is a man who does not back down easily. It will take much to break him. The death of his child, perhaps?'

Rachel paled but said nothing.

'You don't know the colonel as well as you think you do,' Hart said grimly. 'You harm his daughter and he'll send an army into these hills to find you and kill you, and he'll never quit until the job's done.'

'That is even better,' said Bidziil. 'Let him come. Let him bring his army. We will join together in one final battle for the future, and the whites will die in such numbers that these hills will be shunned forever.'

Hart shook his head as if to dismiss such a prospect. 'For God's sake, man, see sense! Your people against ours, the

Indian Wars all over again, and no one with a single clear idea what they're fighting and dying for? It doesn't have to come to that, not if you can find it in your heart to trust us to do the right thing.'

'And your 'right thing'?' said Bidziil. 'You tell your people there is nothing here for them, no gold, no silver, no copper or minerals? And you expect them to believe that and leave this place alone? You are truly children.' He shook his head. 'No. My way is better. For who is there to care when an ordinary man dies? But when the daughter of a *rich* man dies . . . that is the spark that will bring about the final battle.'

'Don't do this, Old One,' said Hart. 'I beg you.'

'*You* will live,' Bidziil said, as if that were meant to comfort him. 'You will take her corpse back to her father, and he will see what his greed has cost him. And then there will be war.'

His right hand vanished into the folds of his coat, and when it came back out the fingers were curled around the handle of a long hunting knife.

Realizing there was no reasoning with him Hart did the only thing he could. He lunged forward and punched the old man hard in the face. Bidziil staggered and stumbled backward. But he was tough. Shaking his head to clear it, he came right back at him with the blade raised high.

Hart caught the wrist of his knife-hand, squeezed and bent it backward. Pain made Bidziil gasp. His lidded, rheumy eyes went wide. The knife dropped from his hand, clattered against the cave floor.

He tried to claw at Hart's eyes with the fingers of his free hand. He was no longer an old man, but a cougar, attacking with every ounce of strength in him. Hart eluded his grasp, then stepped close and buried his right fist in the old Indian's stomach. Bidziil's breath left him in a stale rush. Hart hit him again, alongside the head, and the old Navajo went down and stayed there.

Rachel stared at him through large, scared eyes. 'Is he . . . ?'

Hart shook his head. 'He'll live. But we need to be a long way from here before he regains consciousness.'

She didn't need to ask why; the answer was all too obvious. 'Maii',' she whispered.

'Maii',' he confirmed. 'The minute he comes round, he'll summon the shape-shifter again. And he won't stop until he's killed us.'

'Then let's go.'

'Wait,' he said. Bending, he picked up the blackened length of wood next to the flute.

'What's that?'

'I'm not sure,' Hart said. 'But if it's what I think it is, it might come in handy before we're out of these hills.'

24

Hart thought they'd feel safer when the sun came up again. If anything, they felt even more exposed.

Earlier they'd left the mine behind them and, after scanning the area beyond the cave entrance for sign of Maii', finally stepped back out into the chilly night. Hart's head had started pounding again. He tried to ignore it, hoping it would go away.

While Rachel kept watch, he collected up everything he felt they might need for the return journey — mostly just the water skins and a few supplies. Then they set out on the first leg of their dangerous moonlit descent to lower ground.

It was a long night. With only the stars to guide them, they kept descending as fast as they dared, rarely stopping to rest and catch their breath. Maii' was out here somewhere. When he returned to the mine and discovered Bidziil unconscious, or when Bidziil came to and summoned him, it would go bad for them. Very bad.

'H-how much of a head-start do you suppose we have?' Rachel asked.

Hart shrugged. 'I don't know. Twelve hours, if we're lucky. That's why we've got to make them count.'

'What happens . . . you know . . . when Maii' catches up?'

'*If* Maii' catches up,' he said to make her feel better, though both of them knew there was no doubt that he would. 'We do the only thing we can do, Rae. We stand and fight.'

'And how long do you suppose *that* fight'll last?'

'You might be surprised.'

'If you have a plan, now would be a . . . a great time to share it.'

'I'm working on it,' he said. 'Now, watch where you put your feet.'

Now, at sunrise, they were both close to collapse. They'd just gone twenty-four hours without sleep and were finally reaching the end of their reserves. Hart, his eyes scratchy in the light of the new day, saw the Navajo burial-village in the

201

distance and couldn't believe they'd covered such little ground.

He increased their downward pace. Beside him, he could sense Rachel flagging with every step. At last she stopped dead in her tracks and said: 'I . . . I'm sorry, Jase. I can't go on. I can't.'

He looked at her. She stood with her shoulders slumped, arms hanging loose at her sides, shirt and pants covered with a fine scrim of dust. Her hair hung lank, her eyes seemed to have sunk back into her head.

'All right,' he said. 'We'll rest up for a while.'

He gently led her into the shade thrown by one of the hogans. She sank gratefully to her knees. He held one of the skins to her lips and she drank until the water spilled down her dusty chin. He watched as her head sank forward and her breathing grew heavy and slow.

He rubbed his gritty eyes and wondered how this would end. Would Maii' come charging over that far rise, galloping in for the kill on all fours? Was he already here somewhere, just waiting for them to walk right into his trap?

He looked down at the stick he'd taken from Bidziil's cave. It might prove to be the deciding factor in all of this. But any weapon was only as good as the man wielding it. Hart had made it his purpose in life to study almost everything he encountered with equal fervor. It was how he'd learned to speak Italian, how he had become so familiar with Navajo legends and customs. He knew something of magic, but a little knowledge was a dangerous thing. If he got it wrong, that knowledge might as easily kill them as save them.

Again he gazed toward the far rise. Where was Maii' right now? And Bidziil? Was he nursing a sore head at this very minute, and consoling himself with thoughts of what would happen when Maii' caught up with them?

He listened to the morning breeze, half-expecting at any moment to hear the flute-that-wasn't-a-flute, or the thin wail of Harmonica's mouth organ rising up from the pit in the center of the village.

He heard nothing. The silence gave him

a chance to clear his tired mind and think. He tried to remember everything he'd ever learned about the Navajo that might help them now.

It was only a matter of time before Maii' caught up to them. So that was his priority, then — to buy them more time.

He stood up and scanned their surroundings. He needed cedar wood. Cedar was important to the Navajo, as often used for its healing properties as it was for its ability to ward off bad spirits. But it quickly became apparent that there were no cedars in the vicinity.

Then he spotted a cluster of Rocky Mountain juniper on the slopes to the east. Cedar was part of the juniper family. That was something else he'd learned in his endless acquisition of knowledge. He could only hope the link between species was close enough to make this work.

Somehow he summoned the strength to jog out to the trees, where he used his pocket knife to hack away a long strip of bark. This he carried back to the Hogan. Hunkering down he carved a long horizontal gouge in the dirt. When he'd finished making the image he needed, he set about slicing up the bark and stuffing it into the shape, then gently brushing dirt back over the edges to hold everything in place.

For a while he worked so diligently that he forgot just how bone-tired he was. When he was finished, he surveyed his handiwork and hoped that it would work.

Then he too slept.

★   ★   ★

When he woke an hour later, Rachel was looking down at the image he'd created. She turned as he got up and said: 'What's this?'

It was a rough impression of an arrow about eight feet long, with the tip pointing off to the left.

'It's a Navajo spell that wards off evil,' he said.

Her eyes widened. 'Will it work?'

'Let's hope so,' he said. 'Ideally the bark should have been crushed. The best I could do was cut it into pieces. But at the very least it might buy us some time, until Maii' figures out how he can get past it.' He straightened up. 'How do you feel?'

She summoned a smile. 'Better.'

'Then let's get going.'

★ ★ ★

Late that afternoon Hart glanced back over one shoulder and saw that the sky had darkened to a weird shade of purple. A few minutes later there came a harsh, electrical buzz of sound and for just a moment their shadows leapt ahead of them. They stopped and turned just as another jagged fork of lightning speared the earth about three miles away. Rachel looked at Hart and said: 'Tell me that's just a normal storm.'

Lightning continued to stilt-walk across the horizon, flickering down from a sky heavy with pink-bellied clouds. 'I wish I could,' he replied.

They pushed on.

25

Rain lashed the plains behind them. From a distance it looked just like dark, rolling mist. But they didn't look back any more than they had to. If Hart was right, the storm was more than just an expression of Maii's rage at being held back by the arrow charm. The rain would eventually wash all traces of that charm away, and then Maii' would be free to move forward and continue the chase.

Hart concentrated on the journey that still lay before them and hoped Rachel had the good sense to do likewise. The storm seemed to galvanize them, remind them — as if they needed reminding — of what lay behind them.

Ahead, there were also plenty of reminders. They passed them, one at a time. Here was the pass where Harmonica had vanished, the spot where Harmonica had spoken with the Indian girl Hart himself had been unable to see.

Somewhere along the way they skirted the bowl of land that was filled with old human bones, the tree that had burst into flames and almost cost Harmonica his life long before Maii' snatched him away and threw his dead body into the pit, there to await a reunion with his old friend, Corrigan.

Eventually exhaustion hit them again and they had no choice but to find a sheltered spot and rest up. Night fell. It was ominously quiet now that the storm had finally worn itself out. Hart wondered whether or not his charm was still holding Maii' back, or if even now the shape-shifter was stalking down out of the high country, little more than an oily shadow closing the gap between them with every enormous footstep.

When Hart awoke the following dawn he was amazed to find that they were still alive. They rummaged around in their packs, found something they could eat on the move and doggedly continued their descent.

They were in the foothills that yielded to a vast tract of desert now. By the middle of the afternoon they descended a serried amber slope between the buttes where Corrigan had encountered Maii', and Maii' had scratched his throat.

Here Rachel flopped down like a rag doll and again said she could go no farther. Hart threw a fearful glance back in the direction from which they'd just come, half-expecting to see Maii' watching them. As near as he could tell, they were alone.

'Rae,' he said, breathing heavily, 'you don't have any choice. We have to keep going.'

She couldn't even raise her head. 'But I'm just so *tired*, Jase.'

He didn't really know what to say to her, and never got the chance to find out. Even as he opened his mouth, a long, low rumble of thunder rolled down out of the high country.

That made Rachel look up, and when she did she saw the same thing Hart saw — that there wasn't a cloud in the sky.

'Maii',' she whispered.

He nodded. 'He's coming.'

★   ★   ★

The narrow gorge through which a shallow stream reflected sunlight like spilled trinkets opened up ahead of them. Hart grabbed Rachel's hand, pulled her to her feet and half-dragged her toward it.

'C-can't you set another . . . charm?' she asked.

'I don't think there's enough time,' he said honestly. 'But I'm going to finish this once and for all, Rae. That I promise you.'

'How? How can you finish it? You said Maii' was immortal, that he can't be killed.'

'He can't.'

'Then — ?'

There came another rumble of thunder from out of the clear blue sky behind them, followed this time by something else.

A long, menacing, growling howl.

Hart pushed Rachel ahead of him. 'Go! Quickly now!'

She shook her head. 'I can't — '

He grabbed her and got in her face.

'You don't have any *choice*, Rae, not if you want to go on living!'

Her face screwed up, as if to cry. But no tears came. He realized that she was too tired even to cry.

'Listen to me!' he hissed. 'My car and your truck are at the other end of this gorge! If we can reach them before Maii' gets here, we might still be able to outrun him!'

That seemed to get through to her. Her gray eyes cleared a little and deep within them he saw a flicker of hope.

'Now, *move!*' he ordered.

Only God knew how she did it, but she did.

★   ★   ★

Occasionally stumbling on the carpet of loose shale with which the sloping side of the gorge was littered, Rachel tried to ignore all the protestations of her aching body and focus on what lay at the far end of the defile — escape. The urge to look back was almost overpowering, but she knew she must resist it. To slip or fall now would be to seal their fate once and for all.

There came another growl of thunder, another animalistic howl — closer now. She felt Hart push her in the small of the back and somehow she found it within herself to move even faster. Stupidly, a part of her was still insisting that none of this was real, that it was just one long nightmare from which she would awake at any moment. But the fear raging through her was real enough, as was the pain she felt at the thought of never seeing her father again —

Without warning the gorge opened out onto the shelf of land where they'd left the car and trucks. She heard someone sob, realized dimly that the sound had come from her own fear-constricted throat and stumble-ran toward the truck.

'No!' Hart yelled. 'My car — it'll be faster!'

She changed direction. Moments later she fell against the side of the bottle-green Ford, gulping down great draughts of air.

'Get behind the wheel!' Hart told her.

He wrenched open the driver's-side door and grabbed the starter handle from under the seat.

She stared helplessly at him. 'I don't know how to drive!'

'You don't have to! Look, just — '

He felt the next rumble of thunder in his teeth, and this time there was no doubt about it — the howl that followed it was definitely closer.

He drew a breath. 'When the engine turns over, pull out the choke. That's this button here. At the same time you do that you pull back on the throttle, here, and then hit the start button. Can you remember that?'

'I . . . I think so.'

'All right — get ready.'

He went around to the front of the car, inserted the starter handle and gave it a turn. Nothing happened. He looked up and saw Rachel's bloodless face watching him through the windscreen. All at once she looked so young, so scared, so vulnerable.

He turned the handle again. The Ford rocked on its springs and the engine gave a short-lived cough, as if it were clearing its throat.

Behind him he heard another mixture of growl and howl. He had heard wolves many times on his travels, but never so loud. He looked back over one shoulder, thought he glimpsed a shadow sliding along the gorge wall like black grease, even saw it reflected in the shallow stream beneath it and then turned his attention back to the car.

He turned the handle again, this time clenching his teeth and putting every ounce of strength still left in him behind the turn.

The engine roared to life. Hart fell back from it, starter handle in hand, and yelled: 'Pull out the choke and pull back the throttle!' He could see her flustering with the controls. 'That's it! Now press the starter button!'

Just when he thought the engine was going to die on them it seemed to calm and run smoothly. 'You've done it!' he shouted, and started back around the car.

Rae screamed.

Instinctively he twisted around and saw

at once that the very thing he'd feared had finally come to pass.

Maii' was racing along the gorge, howling loud enough to deafen them, jaws open wide so they could see his long yellow teeth dripping saliva.

Maii' was ready to kill.

26

For one stretched moment Hart was transfixed by the sight. Maii' stood ten or twelve feet tall, a loose-limbed giant composed of gray bones that were at once both human and animal. His head was long and sleek, with large eye sockets gaping on either side of a sloping, blunt-ended snout.

He suddenly reared up and his skeletal forepaws flexed in anticipation of the killing to come. In that instant his resemblance to a man was undeniable. He was draped in wolf pelts that swung loosely with his every movement.

Then he dropped back to all fours and continued running straight toward them, water from the stream splashing up around him like molten silver.

'Jase!'

Rachel's voice interrupted Hart's thoughts. Incredibly he took a step toward the oncoming nightmare and threw the starter handle at it. The handle bounced off one broad, bony shoulder and flew end over end into the brush.

As Rachel hunched over in the passenger seat, Hart jumped in behind the wheel. Ahead, through the windshield, the onrushing Maii' rapidly grew larger and larger —

Hart released the brake, stamped his foot down on the accelerator and the little green Model T leapt forward like a goosed racehorse.

As Maii' came blurring out of the gorge Hart aimed the car directly at him. Beside him Rachel screamed. Hart ignored her and kept the car barreling forward.

Maii' saw the vehicle coming and again reared up onto his gaunt back legs.

Hart stamped his foot even harder on the pedal, the car smashing into Maii' and knocking him off his feet. He slammed onto the ground with a rattle of heavy bones.

Hart yanked the wheel, thrust into reverse and collided with the raging giant again before he could get up.

Maii' fell backward, snarling. Hart coolly slipped the gear shift into first and the Model T spun around and away, through the timber and on toward the camp where the colonel's men had been slaughtered.

Rachel swung around in her seat so that she could see through the small rear window.

'What's happening?' he asked without taking his eyes off the blur of trees ahead.

With every fiber in him he wanted her to say that Maii' wasn't moving, he was just sprawled there, finished. But she said: 'Oh God, Jase! He's getting up again! He's coming after us!'

Hart dared to check his side-view mirror. She was right. Maii' was bounding after them like some colossal hound, yapping and snarling as he slowly but steadily gained on them.

Faster, Hart begged the Ford. *Faster! . . . Faster! . . .*

The lightweight vehicle bounced over the uneven ground, ricocheting from one bump to another. Ahead the trees were starting to thin. Then Rachel screamed again and Hart's eyes returned to the rearview mirror.

Maii' was right behind them.

A second later the shape-shifter swiped at the back of the Ford. Something crashed down hard on the roof and it buckled a little. The car itself went down on its springs and then bounced back up again, but kept moving.

'Dammit!' roared Hart. He stamped on the brake, the car wrenched to a halt and Maii', still close and still coming fast, ran right into it. He spilled forward in a loose somersault that took him right over the car and then crashed onto the ground in front of them. Hart put the car into first and drove straight at the creature's large head.

He hit Maii' a grazing blow. It was too much to hope that it would do more than slow him down. But shortly they would be out of the timber and back on the almost non-existent trail, and here they might gain an advantage.

The Ford burst out of the trees and hit the trail with enough force to make it rock and almost roll over onto its side.

'Is he following us?' Hart said.

'No. Do you think you killed him?'

'I can't kill him,' he reminded her. 'No one can. And he won't ever give up.'

'Oh God,' she breathed.

He didn't have to ask what was wrong. He knew. Maii' had just emerged from the trees at a lope and was after them again.

The country was familiar now, if only Rachel had been able to see anything other than the monstrous nightmare that was almost sprinting to catch them up. For mere seconds there was the spot where Tucker, Moore and Ross had died, and Bianchi Battista had lost his sanity, still marked by the colonel's bright blue Studebaker touring car.

Ahead was a bend in the trail, and Maii' was momentarily lost to sight. They drove on. A mile farther and they passed the spot where Harvey Wheeler had emptied the contents of Hart's car into the dirt, hoping to discover who he was and what he wanted here.

Hart didn't slow, just kept going, and then that landmark too vanished.

Maii' came charging around the bend, closing the gap between them with every step, and Rachel felt a scream building in her throat.

'What are we going to do, Jase?' she said desperately.

'Only thing we can do,' he replied as the trail continued to sweep past them on both sides.

'What?'

'The next best thing to killing him,' he murmured cryptically.

27

For one fleeting a moment, as every passing yard brought them closer to their destination, Hart dared to hope that they might just make it. But then the engine coughed and something under the hood dragged ominously. The Model T lurched and then continued to race down through the shouldering hills, following a near-invisible trail that hardly deserved the name.

'What happened?' asked Rachel, alarmed.

He shook his head. 'I don't know. I think we're almost out of gas. There's more in the trunk, but we daren't stop.'

He checked his mirror. Maii' was perhaps half a mile behind them now, but the car was slowing and there was nothing he could do to make it pick up the pace.

'When we stop,' he said, 'I want you to do something for me.'

'What?'

'I want you to get out of here,' he said.

'Run, and keep running, and don't look back. If this works, I'll meet up with you again in Jemez Springs.'

He didn't say anything about if it didn't work.

'I'm not leaving you,' she said.

'It's not up for debate, Rae.'

'But you're bound to need help. You can't fight that thing alone.'

'Rae — '

But that was it — the Model T had given as much as it could. The engine finally spluttered and died, and he turned the wheel to let it coast to a halt beside the trail.

The trail . . .

He realized with a sudden jolt of hope that this might not be over yet, because the car had done its job after all.

'*Run!*' he said, shoving his door open and leaping out.

She got out too, but stared at him and said softly: 'No.'

His whole world seemed to stop turning then. He looked at her and smiled. And somehow she found it within herself to smile back.

Then he grabbed the stick he'd taken from Bidziil's cave. 'At least keep out of sight,' he said.

She watched as he jogged across the other side of the trail, realizing suddenly just where they were. Ignoring his request, she followed him to where he had just stopped and was looking down at the ground.

It was the sand painting that had started this nightmare in the first place.

She looked back down the trail, at Maii', who had slowed to a fluid walk.

'Isn't it about time you told me what we're going to do?' she said.

A drawn-out howl stopped him from replying. As one their heads snapped around and they saw that Maii' had started running again, his wolf pelts hanging and swaying around him.

'We can't kill him,' Hart said without taking his eyes off the shape-shifter. 'But if we're lucky, we can *banish* him.'

As she frowned Hart raised the stick. The sight of it got a reaction from Maii'. Again the giant creature slowed, took a sudden, wary pace back, his skull-head tilted to one side like that of a wary dog. A warning growl vibrated deep inside his heaving chest.

'You see this?' Hart asked Rachel. 'If I'm right, it's a *spirit stick*, fashioned from the wood of a tree that's been struck by lightning. It's big medicine to the Navajo and has many uses . . . including the banishment of evil spirits.'

'What do we do? Point it at him? Use it like some sort of gun?'

'Uh-uh. I'm going to use it like a . . . an amplifier, if you like. Provided I can remember the ritual, the spirit stick should give it extra power and — '

'He's coming,' she said anxiously.

She was right. Maii' was hurrying toward them in a series of long, determined strides, his claws clacking and stretching, his mouth opening and closing, his head seeming to sink into his shoulders in such a way that made him look, in that moment, more animal than human.

'Take cover behind the car,' Hart told her. He then dropped to his knees before the sand painting, held the stick at arm's-length and tried to remember the ritual.

But it had been years since he'd last spoken to a Navaho shaman about it and for one awful moment his mind was a blank —

Maii' broke into a run.

Hart lifted his head to the sky and said: *'Spirits of dragons old and wise . . . Cruise again across the skies . . . Move with love and move with grace . . . Stir the winds within this place . . .'*

He looked around, waited.

Nothing happened.

He tightened his grip on the spirit stick, called again: *'Spirits of dragons old and wise . . . Cruise again across the skies . . . Move with love and move with grace . . . Stir the winds within this place . . .'*

The thudding of heavy paws, the panting of gigantic lungs, the clacking of claws big enough and sharp enough to tear him apart —

Fighting the urge to flee, Hart continued to kneel there, repeating: *'Spirits of dragons old and wise . . . Cruise again across the skies . . . Move with love and move with grace . . . Stir the winds within this place . . . '*

He thought of Tom Ross, whose head had been sheared off, of Perry Tucker, who'd been disemboweled. He thought of Lester Moore and his snapped neck, of Bianchi, driven hopelessly insane.

'Spirits of dragons old and wise . . . Cruise again across the skies . . . Move with love and move with grace . . . Stir the winds within this place . . . '

Closer now, closer . . . and still nothing was happening.

In his mind he saw Harmonica Jones with his hands still clasping his mouth organ, and his head facing the wrong way. He saw Corrigan, with his broken legs buckled beneath him and his guts eaten away, Harvey Wheeler, his face chewed off —

'Spirits of dragons old and wise . . . Cruise again across the skies . . . Move with love and move with grace . . . Stir the winds within this place . . . '

Maii' was almost upon him.

Then it suddenly hit Hart.

Rising to face Maii', he shouted: *'Rise*

with a howl, Feathered Dragon of the Whispering Winds!'

That did it.

Maii' stopped dead in his tracks, only a few strides from him now. The giant, hideous incarnation snarled with rage, and Hart smelled the sour, dead breath he expelled.

Then a breeze picked up and began to swirl the loose sand at Hart's feet. As he took a backward step the breeze strengthened and Hart saw it make Maii's covering of pelts flap and snap.

Maii' snarled again and started forward.

Hart, the spirit stick still in hand, backed toward the car. Above them the sky darkened, moving from pale powder blue to azure, from azure to cobalt, from cobalt to an unsettling shade of iris. It was almost like watching day change to night within a matter of seconds.

And all the time, the wind kept strengthening, strengthening, and even as it tore Hart's hat from his head, it tore also at Maii'. The shape-shifter leaned into it, but it was all he could do to remain standing.

Hart collapsed beside Rachel. Her arms went around him, and held tight. She said something, but her words were whipped away by the gale that was now blowing around them.

Lightning slashed at the sky, great, swollen bolts of it. There may have been thunder, but if there was it couldn't be heard above the roar of the wind.

'Jase!'

Hart heard that much, looked at Rachel, saw that her eyes had widened and turned to see what it was.

A great, whirling funnel of wind and sand had appeared over the ridge to their left. At first glance it looked like a tornado as it spun diagonally across the slope and inexorably toward the sand painting. And yet it was like no tornado Hart had ever witnessed before. It was crazy to even think it, but the column seemed to have intent ... purpose ... and nothing would make it change the course upon which it was set.

Maii' roared defiantly as the twisting maelstrom edged ever closer to the sand painting. He batted at the air with his bony claws, but it did no good. This was no wind of nature's making. This had come from elsewhere.

Hart and Rachel watched in morbid fascination as its swirling, narrow lower end finally touched the edge of the painting. At once all the colors mixed and blurred, crushed gypsum combining with yellow ochre, red sandstone and charcoal merging to make something that looked unsettlingly like an enormous smear of dark blood. And then brightly-colored flower pollen swirling, swirling —

Maii' gave one last, tortured howl of fury and then he began to *stretch*, as if being pulled toward the heart of the tornado that wasn't a tornado at all. The bones from his outstretched hands-that-were-paws, paws-that-were-hands began to pull apart, link by link, and fly into the rotating funnel like iron filings attracted to a magnet. The bones of his arms followed on, his skull, his ribs, pelvis, legs and feet, all flying into that raging windstorm. His pelts were flung to the ground; and then, in a sudden burst of light that could have been an explosion but carried with it no sound, they too vanished.

Holding tight to each other, Hart and Rachel watched as the moving tornado climbed the rise again, slowly but still with purpose. It reached the ridge, vanished beyond it, and then, only then, the wind began to die down, the sky to brighten again from its unsettling shade of iris back to pale powder blue

Rachel sagged in Hart's arms. It was over.

Almost.

28

The silence was deafening, but no longer oppressive. It was, Hart told himself, just about the most blessed sound — or lack of it — he'd ever heard.

It was a long time before Rachel finally let him go and stood back. She looked absolutely exhausted and yet at the same time incredibly, undeniably beautiful.

'Is it over?' she dared ask. Her voice was hoarse, her throat dry.

'For now, at least,' Hart replied.

'But for you, it goes on?' It wasn't really a question, even though she gave it that intonation. 'You're still willing to go where the dark is darkest, after this?'

'*Especially* after this,' he replied. 'But it won't be easy, Rae. Not if it means leaving you behind.'

'If it's any consolation,' she whispered, and looked away from him while she composed herself, 'the feeling's mutual.'

He wanted to kiss her, but knew that

now was not the time. Everything they had witnessed, everything they'd experienced, was still too fresh.

Instead he said: 'Are you still going to tell your father that the mine's played out?'

She nodded. 'I'm sick of these mountains, and I want nothing of the treasure they contain.' She looked around. 'We won, didn't we? Against Maii', I mean?'

'Yes — this time.'

'But there have been too many deaths along the way to make me feel anything like a winner. If others want to try their luck up here ... ' Her smile was short-lived and immensely sad. ' ... it's their funeral,' she finished.

Hart didn't say anything.

Rachel looked at him, saw that he was admiring her and said: 'Don't tell me — there's hope for me yet — *Jase!*'

He reacted immediately, turned on one heel just as Bidziil launched himself from where he'd been crouching on the blind side of the car, his hunting knife held high over his gray head. He screamed something — God alone knew what — and his tarnished medals flopped and bounced against the material of his old frock coat as he launched his attack.

Instinctively Hart dodged to one side. The blade of the hunting knife stabbed at the roof of the Ford and snapped in half. But Bidziil wasn't about to let that stop him. He hurled himself at Hart again, the jagged blade raised to strike, and Hart brought up the only thing he could possibly use as a weapon — the spirit stick.

In his fury, Bidziil ran straight onto the point and screamed.

At first the stick met with some resistance. Then it punched out of Bidziil's back in a red spray. The old shaman's fathomless eyes bugged wide. He looked into Hart's face without seeing it and his mouth started working as he sought to sing his death-song.

He collapsed at Hart's feet and died before the first word could leave his lips.

★ ★ ★

Hart slumped back against the car, suddenly weaker than he'd ever been before. Rachel came to him, held him, stared down at the dead Navajo.

'Now it's over,' she whispered.

She was right, he thought. Or was she? As Hart looked at Bidziil, he thought about what the shaman had told them back in the mountains. *This land will suffer an unhappy fate, that it will bear a terrible, destructive fruit, unless I can keep the white man away from it.*

What had he meant by that?

Wondering if he would ever find out, he held Rachel tight and said: 'I hope so, Rae. I really, truly hope so.'

THE END

235

Authors' Note

In the early years of World War II, the United States government decided to build an atomic bomb in order to counter the threat posed by Germany, who was at that time also trying to develop a nuclear capability. Originally known as Project Y, the work would be eventually be classified at an *Above Top-Secret* level.

In order to maintain this secrecy, the work had to be conducted in an area that offered isolation, privacy and, for obvious reasons, a moderate climate. The scientific director of the project, Robert Oppenheimer, also requested a laboratory that was set in beautiful surroundings that would inspire his team.

On November 25 1942 they finally settled on a plateau a little over five miles east of the Jemez Mountains. It was called Los Alamos.

The rest, as they say, is history.

We do hope that you have enjoyed reading this large print book.

Did you know that all of our titles are available for purchase?

We publish a wide range of high quality large print books including:
Romances, Mysteries, Classics
General Fiction
Non Fiction and Westerns

Special interest titles available in large print are:
The Little Oxford Dictionary
Music Book, Song Book
Hymn Book, Service Book

Also available from us courtesy of Oxford University Press:
Young Readers' Dictionary
(large print edition)
Young Readers' Thesaurus
(large print edition)

For further information or a free brochure, please contact us at:
Ulverscroft Large Print Books Ltd.,
The Green, Bradgate Road, Anstey,
Leicester, LE7 7FU, England.
Tel: (00 44) **0116 236 4325**
Fax: (00 44) **0116 234 0205**

FOREIGN ASSIGNMENT

Sydney J. Bounds

In the unstable Congo region of Africa, the state of Katanga is an oasis of calm. President Tshombe and his government are united; the country's mines and industries supply the West with copper and uranium. But others, who stand to benefit if the government go under, have plans to assassinate the President. Meanwhile, Detective Simon Brand must prevent the assassination and root out the men behind the plot — and he has just seventy-two hours in which to do it . . .

MOTIVE FOR MURDER

John Russell Fearn

Inspector Mallison was reluctant to arrest the murdered man's son, although the incriminating evidence was overwhelming: he'd been alone with his father immediately prior to the murder and there'd been a bitter quarrel; Goldstein was killed trying to alter his will — unfavourably for his son; the weapon, a desk paperweight bore the son's fingerprints, and his father had withdrawn financial support for a new West End play in which his son was to star. Yet still Mallinson wasn't convinced . . .